T0194927

The Valet

aka
The Adventures of Will Ferrell and the Scandinavian

Book 1 of,
The Hollywood movie/TV series version

BRYAN FLETCHER

authorHOUSE®

AuthorHouse™
1663 Liberty Drive
Bloomington, IN 47403
www.authorhouse.com
Phone: 1 (800) 839-8640

Published by AuthorHouse 07/24/2019

ISBN: 978-1-7283-2020-5 (sc)
ISBN: 978-1-7283-2018-2 (hc)
ISBN: 978-1-7283-2019-9 (e)

Library of Congress Control Number: 2019910164

Print information available on the last page.

CHAPTER 10, Part 3: Then a person may seriously consider		
CHAPTER 11, Part 1: Dog		
CHAPTER 11, Part 2		
CHAPTER 11, Part 3		
CHAPTER 11, Part 4: Proper treatment	Same-old, same-old human tendencies, a vast collection of things including words, yet an exceptionally poor ability to communicate with other humans and their animal neighbors	
CHAPTER 11, Part 5		
CHAPTER 12, A tiny sparrow		
CHAPTER 13, Part 1: A Nobel Committee member, Swedish Academy committee secretary, and permanent seasoned adviser		
CHAPTER 13, Part 2		
CHAPTER 13, Part 3		
CHAPTER 14: Intermission		
CHAPTER 15		
CHAPTER 16		
CHAPTER 17: The duck, dog, and tiny sparrow puzzle among each other	The conscious and spirit gradually unfolds, an evolution, a legato, blank verse, or metrical, and rise oh noble spirit, rise, rise!	
CHAPTER 18, Part 1	Golden age of humans?	

CHAPTER 28: The crowd includes 1) a famous dog whisperer, 2) professional notetaker for very wealthy college legacy students, 3) fortune cookie writer who really hates cookies and is dressed as a philosopher of science, Gottfried Wilhelm (von) Leibniz, 4) *cicisbeismo*, 5) famous drug dealer, 6) scruffy professional street beggar, 7) illegal immigrant with colorful t-shirt that proudly says so on both sides, and 8) opera singer dressed as Giuseppe Fortunino Francesco Verdi?	Is it ok to step on the ant, or hit a monkey and win a cookie?	
CHAPTER 29: Intermission: Son of Dave, "Old Times Were Good Times"?		
CHAPTER 30, Part 1: Is it ok to kiss a puppy?	And something else, heaven on earth?	
CHAPTER 30, Part 2		
CHAPTER 30, Part 3		
CHAPTER 31, Part 1: Do fashionistas and hauterflies have a vital function?		
CHAPTER 31, Part 2		
CHAPTER 31, Part 3		
CHAPTER 31, Part 4		
CHAPTER 31, Part 5		
CHAPTER 32		

CHAPTER 42, Part 6		
CHAPTER 42, Part 7		
CHAPTER 42, Part 8: At that crowd Manhattan accident, around a dead Will Ferrell, aka David, and *Erika Segersäll Unræd*, the Scandinavian, unusual air swirls, then smells of sycamore, birch, and mulberry		
CHAPTER 42, Part 9		A 200,000-year search, and those events, for another below-average quality grubstake, sold at an above-average price
CHAPTER 42, Part 10		
CHAPTER 42, Part 11: Publisher note: A chapter component, deliberately withheld by the writer		
CHAPTER 42, Part 12: Konark Sun Temple, thirteenth-century, India	a throne, "the Nth Degree," for a hero with a thousand faces	Mostly hidden. And it's a "Long way back home"
CHAPTER 42, Part 13		The crown and throne system seems older that dirt, the Iron Age, Bronze Age, Golden Age of Great Apes, likely older than an eon, older than the universe, a beach-sized thing

CHAPTER 42, Part 14, A: Indirect story side note: Someone, tribe, or coalition of, deliberately herds war refugees into another peaceful community	Say their collective name, and they swam	
CHAPTER 42, Part 14, B		
CHAPTER 42, Part 15: In back of this throne system, from a central section, a toddler emerges and waddles about, one throne system feature after another		
CHAPTER 42, Part 16, A: "I'm going there to see my Father.... And all my loved ones who've gone on...."	419-year sleep, one that started in the year 1600, the end of the European Renaissance, because of the golden age of robber barons	
CHAPTER 42, Part 16, B		
CHAPTER 42, Part 16, C		
CHAPTER 42, Part 17		
CHAPTER 42, Part 18		In general, the universe seems rigged
CHAPTER 42, Part 19: A creature arrives, yet not visible, has no mass, and takes up no space, no volume, yet emits a considerable amount of gravitons and "exotic forms"		

CHAPTER 42, Part 19, B: A young Japanese woman with serious medical problems, terminal, weeks to live	And, this creature wonders why, some Japanese pensioners want to go to jail, and why, the Japan's Princess Ayako surrenders her royal title	
CHAPTER 42, Part 19, C: *If she dies, I die*		
CHAPTER 42, Part 19, D		
CHAPTER 42, Part 19, E		
CHAPTER 42, Part 19, F: And, yet another commercial break, Son of Dave, "Aint Goin To Nike Town"?		
CHAPTER 42, Part 19, G, Intermission, Son of Dave, "Going For Ice, Everyone Back To My Hotel, Ep1"?		
CHAPTER 42, Part 20, H, Intermission, and a different party, everyone is invited, Shaggy featuring Chaka Khan "Get my party on"?		
CHAPTER 42, Part 19, I		

▼

PART 1

"HAVE A NICE DAY."

In Manhattan, New York, Monday, 9:28 a.m., in his ever so cramped bed space under a stairwell, an average guy named Will Ferrell startles to a sitting position, and bumps his temple.

***

Then, not repeating the same foul word, for three straight minutes, as if a true cuss master, he curses words wholly unfit for print, and curses above and beyond everyday foul mouth themes; as a cuss virtuoso, yet high cultural style, within a lowbrow art form, a sweet science of exceptional foul-speak designed to shock and provoke the senses.

***

And yet, if done in a certain way, it reveals a well-seasoned mind; certain refined judgment, sentiment and taste, even scholarship—as odd as that sounds—and with a well-crafted mastery of aesthetics, of nature, art, beauty, taste, and especially the sublime.

***

1

Will Ferrell, yet his real name is David Ferrell?

No, no, no.

David!

Is the only name on his birth certificate, one name, as some people only have one name.

***

Then he rubs his temple, reels, and looks about this cramped apartment: if a person might call it a studio apartment, as it resembles life under a cramped stairwell, and next to the bed is a small faded photograph of an old, dark-blue step van, a multipurpose enclosed motor vehicle.

***

Then he says rest, "Yes, and relax.

"Yes.

"Breathe.

"Yes.

"Really breathe, and lay back.

"Yes.

"Relax, really relax."

CHAPTER 1

▼

PART 2

Yet moments later, his eyes notice a left forearm, *Have a nice day* ☺ Band-Aid, with cotton ball underneath.

And he says, "That seems strange, quite, as I've had no blood taken; none, in the last few years, or more?"

"In fact, these past few years, my health is excellent."

***

Yet moments later, his viewpoint spins…

… Such as, if a long night in a "bar," then one sense of the word after another…

… And the spin matches the long bar, galactic bar, and that universal spin direction, based on location-location-location, of clockwise?

As a result, David says, "I tried to believe, in God, and James Dean."

CHAPTER 1

▼

PART 3

And, in this ever so cramped tiny apartment, he carefully sits, then maneuvers out, to a standing position, seems disoriented, quite, and slowly staggers about, and mumble something, then one ever so complex phrase after another; as if a unique set dynamic, and prime time live!

***

Yet, one phrase after another resembles a financial stock trade, option, and something else, such as one new "super stock" after another, a "total conviction, buy sign," a rare occurrence, one gap-up-stock after another, then another breakout potential, and another; a wide moat, greatly undervalued, and one heavily leveraged option position after another.

***

And he also says, one phrase after another, as if complex mathematics; applied in one area of mathematics after another, abstract and concrete, abstract object theory, abstract particulars, concrete, spatiotemporal entities, type–token distinction, exonumia, numismatic item, object, token, medal, script, or combination of, such as infinitary combinatorics, probabilistic forecasting, ensemble forecasting, and a game theory; gamification, bundle theory, as if the ultimate metagame, an experimental Delphic-Bayesian game theory expanse, supreme, universal metastack yet, another thing; supremely indescribable.

***

Yet he says all, as if a single unified wave function, a unified theory of, and mostly a hidden ontic wave, unusual universal hydrodynamics Rayleigh-Taylor instability, with projection of products, greater swirl of fractured turmoil, with other products, steps, and things.

***

Or say another way, quite disoriented, and while he slowly staggers about, David mumbles one phrase after another, an econometric index by time series of the long game, of differential games, such as the continuous pursuit and evasion, and the play of one game develops the rules for another game, of which shows as complex nested local and worldwide clusters?

***

Such as, each contains a mission, design, function, content, timing, and so forth, as if one ultimate insider strategy guide after another; with ever so serious "ways and means," yet something else, something.

***

And what he says resembles one investment first mover advantage effort after another, of one gap up stock worth grabbing, such as one "penny stock most explosive" after another, a future ten bagger or more, such as a truly great treasure, a sigma function.

Yet, as if foreshadowing a major event, the future, a fifty-first USA state, the ultimate, supreme IPO, five trillion dollars or more, that folds more than willing unincorporated places, places corporate and various local, state, and federal government often neglect, again, and again, year after year, and decades, such as all those broken promises.

And this event, ever so reasonably and discreetly folds Canada into it as a super state, and far more powerful than "Wall Street and other major financial markets" could ever imagine, such as Sheryl Crow's "Long Way Back," the Official Video."

▼

PART 4

Then eight seconds later, the Dow Jones Industrial Average instantaneously leaps up, three percent, then moments later, a bit more, and another, as if a massive wave of prosperity; just like that: a major lift!

▼

PART 5

AND YET ANOTHER A COMMERCIAL BREAK, ANOTHER BIG BANG, AND "BABY YOU KNOW ME"

And, say as if, "Baby You Know Me, Wolfsuka?"

CHAPTER 2

▼

Then, David seriously staggers about the room wearing 100 percent comfy, cotton pajamas, bottoms loosely fitted, string waist, and shirt that boldly says, "I Love Scandinavia," front and back, overlaid with different pictures, seen below, and each picture, has nation-state flags of Denmark, Norway, Sweden, then for some reason has it Finland and Iceland, all the Nordic countries, then Norwegian islands of Svalbard and Jan Mayen, Greenland, the Faroe Islands, and other islands; that all in all, to some people seem as if a considerable stretch.

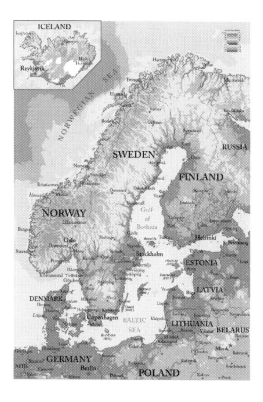

***

Then, one of his Hello Kitty slippers trips on the carpet edge, and that chain of events.

***

And, as he stumbles, then falls out the Manhattan apartment window, a minor pajama thread snags on something.

CHAPTER 3

▼

Then moments later, that thread causes an entanglement, as if a typical phenomenon, a minor thing could create a major event.

***

And in this case, it causes a nearby table apartment compact disk (CD) to flip about the apartment.

And the title seems, ever so allusive.

***

Yet the CD eventually impacts a "classic history of world literature" bookshelf edge, and leaves a mark on a CD song, "Traveling Man, John Brown's Body, *Spirits All Around Us*"?

CHAPTER 4

▼

AND HIS FALL SEEMS, TO LAST FOREVER.

CHAPTER 5

▼

BLANK

▼

INTERMISSION, PART 1

CHAPTER 6

▼

INTERMISSION, PART 2

Then, two, three, four!

CHAPTER 7

▼

PART 1

ERIKA SEGERSÄLL UNRÆD, THE SCANDINAVIAN

Eventually, and belly first, David lands in a considerable shrub, bounces out, wildly tumbles high in a considerable arc, and lands in the middle of a dense Manhattan morning rush-hour crowd, on top of woman named *Erika Segersäll Unræd*, the Scandinavian, who falls back, with his face onto her most sensitive "area," a source and potential of all civilizations.

***

And a major side note, the area best not mentioned in great detail; as here and now, a young reader may receive a true shock.

CHAPTER 7

▼

PART 2

A READER SIDE NOTE, ESPECIALLY TO A YOUNG READER

And with that, a young reader may spark one major realization after another, some indirect, yet with ever so serious implications, then one new mental connection after another.

***

Such as, the obvious, of "Oh my!" his face presses into her most sensitive area.

Then, the young reader may connect one thought after another, may connects the dots.

***

Connect the history, of what people did and said, such as one crude sly comment and joke after another, that hints at the "classic and salacious." And, based on a surge of hormones, from that special DNA brew, and the urgent need to merge with the sublime aspect of eternity, of which represents no small achievement.

***

As often, a very young person cannot fully fathom lust; and how that major disability, can lead to lechery, and can corrupt one everyday word or thing after another.

So much so, everyday life takes on a shocking new perspective.

***

And of greater importance, the young reader may eventually realize; all humans are born too soon.

Born too fragile, vulnerable, and lack a historical context of true danger, the human species, DNA, microbiome, and biome, that often delivers an ever so slow ability to mature.

***

As infants and toddlers have few options, such obey or else; yet need so many more meaningful, easy, effective, and efficient linguistic options.

***

So infants and toddlers do not have to rely on, a cry equivalent of: SOS, abandon ship, abandon ship!

▼

PART 3

A READER SIDE NOTE, ESPECIALLY TO A YOUNG READER

And also, this fragility seems especially true, before a child first touches earth, such as with a foot, toe, palm, right index finger, or "left" material index.

***

And often, a child needs an additional nine months or so, and official preschool-age skills advantages.

Or better yet, a human needs to be born with the skills of age eight, sixteen, or better yet, a thirty-two-year-old, well-seasoned mind.

***

As, the history of the human species and mammals, relative to their life span, shows an ever so slow development rate; a maturation, and ready for the ultimate ritualized act of mature content, to become the vehicle of life, the possibility as a founder, to create a truly great civilization.

CHAPTER 8

▼

And this impact by David, causes this national Scandinavian poet, a specialist of intangible cultural heritage, a Manhattan woman named *Erika Segersäll Unræd*, to fall on her back and drop an unusual heavily ornate, fully inscribed, in great detail, as if a universal translator, yet birch-bark drink container, filled with a morning liquid breakfast concoction, of myrtle, cranberry, honey, and medicinal ingredients, that sprays in her eyes, and on hair, hands, clothing, and shoes with serious implications.

***

However, and of greater importance, both of these people seem knocked out, completely.

***

And a closer look at her implies, she is a jaded aristocratic Manhattanite.

***

And she seems as if a history of the true classics, with her neatly pressed Scandinavian outfit, made of the finest material, that seems ancient in style, yet an exceptionally fashion forward statement, a unique, "vernacular architecture," a style based on local needs, availabilities, reflecting local traditions, ever so fit, and timeless, at one angle after another.

***

Of which, it shows a certain thematic thrift, yet elegant; quite.

And, it resembles an ever so sophisticated protohistoric Scandinavian outfit, the *Bromme Ahrensburg* culture, a late Upper Paleolithic culture, the *Allerød* Oscillation?

***

Such as, the complete outfit resembles one of the oldest human tribe's sense-of-timeless fashion, with a unique elegant string skirt, short-sleeved shirt, woven belt with a high culture bronze spiked belt disc status symbol, cowhide trim on it, and the entire outfit.

And on her back hangs a neatly folded supplement, a ultra-fine cashmere blanket that easily detaches, to serve as a cold weather option.

For example, if the weather suddenly changes, maybe a wind gust or more, then this supplement provides exceptional protection.

And on the whole, this outfit also seems as if a clear nod to the Egtved Girl, from the Nordic Bronze Age, discovered outside Egtved, Denmark.

***

Of equal importance, here and now, in *Erika*'s drink, there are no smells of liquor, none, yet hinted at before.

***

Such as, before the impact, the crowd notices something, yet thought she has a medical condition, not related to this impact.

And, a quick guess, it seems as if something has damaged her caudate nucleus, subthalamic nucleus, and much more.

For example, when a person quickly scans a situation, for one cue after another, and rapidly summarizes the situation, in totality.

That ability seems damaged, and based on how she previously interacted with other crowd members, one after another, and other nuance things, especially previous commute encounters.

***

So much so, something has damaged her understanding of proxemics, an understanding of physical space to communicate, and chronemics, an understanding of time, as it related to schema, schedule, arrange, and manage communications.

***

And, from a mysterious illness, she seems to have lost these skills, at least according to a few people in the Manhattan crowd, as one by one, they move towards, then surround her and David.

***

And, to the crowd that edges closer to her, all of which seems a bit strange, as no one normally behaved that way.

Especially, as before the accident, *Erika* gave the full impression of, "What have I become," as if lost in Manhattan, New York, in a classic sea of people, yet felt on a stage.

Where she has an identity foreclosure, a major phase transition that tests and puts her identity in full crisis, such as identity versus role crisis of the self, with those mysteries of various internal and external separations, all those nuances.

CHAPTER 9

▼

And within the crowd, someone mumbles her nickname, the original *"Estima."*

Or, did that person say *Aestimare, Aesta or Aristo*?

Or, said another way, from another perspective, people have called her *Mathematica*, as if combinatorial group theory, based on a variation of Banach-Tarski paradox reversed, a full unification philosophy of mathematics, yet as if an artist, an author, maybe the author or auctor of Scandinavian culture finally, fully reemerges; or *Mathematica* as if a typical fresh, cool Scandinavian breeze?

***

However, in this crowd, and one after another, a person mumbles a different nickname based on her personality, of who she really is, such as "Atheltic Dramatica."

"Uppsala."

"Danelagh Atheling."

Yet in the past, her father, mother, brother, sister, and relatives, who live in the homeland, each called her a different nickname, "the Norwegian," "the Swede," "the Dane," the "Scandinavian," and "Ah-renic," as if she symbolizes a great misunderstood rescue specialist, an ever so reliable heuristic, such as wilderness extrication then *apokatastasis*, a reconstitution, restitution, and virtuous restoration of individuals, the social systems, and nature, especially the full Scandinavian diaspora, and any lost souls.

***

And this unusual phenomenon, may account for *Erika Segersäll Unræd*'s ever so serious political problems, of so many people viewing her quite differently, as if a Rorschach Inkblot Test.

And often, nation-states reel at the idea of a full, ever so natural diaspora unification.

***

And of equal importance, in the past, no one seems willing to show proof that she had or is politically undermining any Scandinavian nation-state, such as an agent *provocateur,* a rogue, a Mata Hari, honeypot, *femme fatale;* a female agent using romance to compromise a target, and in this case the entire Scandinavian people and diaspora.

***

Or, say another way, regarding *Erika Segersäll Unræd,* no one offers obvious or subtle proof.

CHAPTER 10

▼

PART 1

And, in this crowd, a widely recognized, Norwegian exile, quite familiar with her situation, quietly whispers to a widely recognized Swedish exile, "Her family lives in Norway.

"Yet long ago, *Erika* was banished, and along one regular, then remote hiking path after another, up and up, into a major vista, and another, then one remote hut system, after another.

***

"Then eventually, *Erika* escaped the country, to another remote hiking path, and another, and remote hut system, then major trail, and another, and up into the majestic mountains with sweeping vista, with an exceptional view of land, sea, air and the heavens.

***

And moments later, the Norwegian exile eyes narrow, as the voice slows, often pauses between phrases, as if admiration, "Yes, a true adventure, a truly great threshold adventure, and her destiny in the monomyth.

***

"And eventually, she arrived in Manhattan, New York, as many of us are here."

***

Then, ever so quietly says with nuance, as if quite thoughtful, of each ever so careful phrase placement, "So much so, and for reasons unclear to most people, however implied, for serious Norway state sovereignty concerns, such as, it directly relates to the Westphalian sovereignty system, a 'physical system', an agreement that respects principle of territorial integrity, the principles of international law that each nation-state has sovereignty over its territory and domestic affairs, to the exclusion of all external powers, on the principle of noninterference in another country's domestic affairs.

"As a result of tremendous pressure, she was not ushered out of Norway; she quietly fled along one hiking trail after another."

And the Swedish exile carefully looks about, then gestures caution.

Then both of them cautiously look about the dense, tremendous crowd for danger.

***

And the Swede carefully, ever so quietly says, often pauses at end of each phrase, "Nowadays, things are not what they appear to be, and are likely one test after another, on regular people with legitimate concerns, and monitored by one hot GPS ready camera and microphone after another, 24/7 through a cell phone, TV remote control, or assistant, an Echo, Apple Siri, Google Assistant, Amazon Alexa, Cortana, or some other construct, maybe a hidden embedded system, that travels everywhere, in the car, work, shop, electronic fitness bracelet, electronic training equipment, home, bathroom, and sleep; with head on pillow, to reveal everything, then sell privacy, to anyone, to sell out: compromise a sacred trust, friendship, and true loyalty, for personal gain; often for a few coins, or thirty pieces of silver.

***

"So much so, most people, seem caught in the middle of one turf war after another, of genders, families, friends, tribes, teams, employers, economic systems, politics, cultures, religions, races, and much more; such as intramural and extramural turf wars, often between powerful corporate interests, yet called government; often corporate interests too big to fail; or, as if yet another fund raising technique, or to justify something.

"For example, a person must live as if corporate and state-bound art, state-dependent memory, and a state-transition equation for status *quo* justification, often with tough love, and yet another corporate, state bureaucratic expansion, entanglement, and mishmash, mostly unseen, such as the real science and "mythology of lost.

"Because, there appear few decent direct routes through life, to reasonable, and the promised land.

***

"Or say another way, all these turf wars and bureaucratic expansions often produce another layer of gnarl, or gristle, of tough, tendinous, or yet another fibrous systems, another entanglement.

"Of which, represents the classic civilization or favorite fund raising tool, to promote impulse, and smolder with a small percent of reasonable options. And they often promote the classic animal, of fight, flight or surrender, or better yet buy, buy into a program or script, then sign a few very complex long-term contracts, with ever so small fine print to entangle.

"And, it puts regular people under considerable stress, pressure point after pressure point that defies common sense and logic, such as inductive, abductive, and deductive; and creates another holy smokes moment, often 'tit for tat,' and 'got yah' for being human, being normal, and 'got yah' based on a technicality, such as something taken out of context, and not perfect, such as perfect thought construction and speech.

"As if a person must serve without significant fault, without a clear reasonable path to the promised land, and away from one weird situation after another, said normal, or law.

"As people are often treated as if mere stagecraft, theatrical scenery, theatrical property, or a principal with the least privilege and relegated a role with an ever so flat script.

"And everyone must live under the intense scrutiny, as if behind the Berlin wall or some other cultural equivalent.

"Live under the bright lights, the Big Show, and prime time live.

"Or say another way, nowadays, many social, commercial, and political systems seem weird, absurd, deliberately made so by these systems, made fake, an ever so common trope, again, the classic set of Machiavellianism techniques, now said *virtù*, as if virtuous, of moral excellence, yet another confidence game, the use of obvious and ever so sly deceit, one conspiracy after another, of gaming the system, the system gaming itself, and crowd manipulations, imply rioting and looting.

"And the news media, and political systems, yet most as mere proxies of powerful hidden interests, often imply, day after day, week after week, year after year, and generations directly say, proclaim the end of days, Four Horsemen of the Apocalypse, fire, brimstone, tremendous suffering and the last few days, the final days; so, as per their request, *Legend of the Mighty Sparrow, Part 3, End of Days, Eschatology, the Final Events of History, the Ultimate Human Destiny, End of Time, and Ultimate Fate of the Universe,* a supreme universal rollback...

***

"... a history of the human species, omnivores, nearly everything is up for grabs, according to their prehistoric brain system, a physical system, and social media control system, deliberately determine to keep it that way, often for a few coins, or thirty pieces of silver, or some other cultural equivalent; often for a below average grubstake, bought at a high price.

"And make these media control system techniques, the linguistic channels into, yet another confidence game, as the new norm, to make divisive and paranoid, and with so many contradictions.

"So, in the middle of yet another said urgent, ominous newscast, political *séance* to contact the living dead party members, or corporate meeting, that cries wolf, again, and demands us, to join the raucous yet again, and pay above average prices for below average results: a normal person might suddenly stand, and say "really, tell me more," then politely excuse themselves, then quietly dropout, move to a great forest, and live off the grid, and make a 100% organic garden, Non GMO, and/or, start a hippy haven, hippie land, the best hippies from A to Z, or go to a drop city.

"Or maybe, travel light, and follow the 'local hippie trail' and live off the land.

"In fact, travel the national hippie trail and beyond, such as from England, Brussels, Luxembourg, and Frankfurt.

"Then travel to Munich, Salzburg, Vienna, and Budapest.

"Then travel to Szeged, Belgrade, Sofia, Istanbul, Ankara, and avoid Tehran, and Lahore.

"Yet stop in Delhi, yes, Goa, Kathmandu, Benares, on the banks of the Ganges, Dhaka, and Bangkok.

"Or consider something else.

"Yes, something different; a person can travel the Banana Pancake Trail, the Banana Pancake Circuit.

"However, it may be best to avoid the Gringo Trail, those classic tourist routes, which have greatly spoiled so many people, places and things, spoiled the culture, such as the Central and South American versions.

"Or, a person could travel the Southern Cross Route.

"If not, try something different, such as travel based on that book, such as, based on the *See the USA the Easy Way, 136 Loop Tours to 1,200 Places, Reader's Digest*, hardcover, April 1, 1995".

Or, something else, maybe travel the "lost sea expedition route, then each lost continent"?

Such as, next time, in the middle of yet another said urgent, ominous newscast, political *séance* to contact the living dead party members, or corporate meeting, that cries wolf, and demands us, to join the raucous yet again, and pay above average prices for below average results.

CHAPTER 10

▼

PART 2

An everyday thing?

And often, for a normal person, it seems as if yet another "same-old, same-old," and maybe a turf war, an ever so tenacious grudge.

Yet often, life seems as if another misadventure, less freedom and high stress in a classic "quagmire" or "trap" in every sense of those two words; a tenacious prickly thing sold as if another illusion, often a same-day in-the-moment illusion or idea of origin, for example the same old story and thematic structure.

So much so, a normal person under tremendous stress may surrender yet again, as they must pay a sizeable debt, and that momentum, purchased at above average prices, yet received below average quality, again.

So, this person may stand up mid meeting, look about as if *déjà vu*, then politely say something, to show a reasonable level of skepticism, resistance, to digging in the same expensive ditch with few living wage features, or dither in a ditch, or is it dithyrambic, to ramble ditched?

So, as a classic cautionary phrase or two, or maybe mid meeting mention a song title, something cultural, and situationally appropriate, maybe "Son of Dave, Ain't Goin to Nike Town"?

CHAPTER 10

▼

PART 3

Or said another way, nowadays, many systems seem weird, quite, and the new norm with one unreasonable situation after another, with divisiveness, paranoia, and so many contradictions that lack logic.

So much so, a person seriously considers: abandon ship, abandon ship!

CHAPTER 10

▼

Part 4, Blank

CHAPTER 11

▼

PART 1

A DOG

Moments later, near that tremendous Manhattan accident crowd, a dog walks itself, again, as certain dogs need no formal license, no local certificate, no new age chip imbedded under the skin, or passport.

Just as importantly, here and now, few people minor question it, mostly a wayward stranger, out of the loop, people out of the loop yet again.

***

So much so, one crowd member after another notices, and minor reels back, as today the dog walks a pet duck, well ahead on long leash.

***

And of equal importance, it does so on a leash that could easily break, as the leash appears symbolic, as if a prophetic, an adaptive regression, or additive contemplative technique.

And that leash has various inscriptions, which include book titles, *Shipwrecks of the Western Hemisphere, Lost Islands* by Henry Stommel, *The Unabridged Devil's Dictionary,* Works by Thomas Babington Macaulay, First Baron Macaulay, *The Sketch Book of Geoffrey Crayon, Gent,* and *10,000 Dreams Interpreted,* Rand Mc Nally," and one algorithm after another, mostly encrypted classified algorithms, as if to taunt the fact no one could crack these techniques, ever, such as never ever!

***

In addition, for other reasons, this Manhattan walk seems quite odd, such as public leash law requires a dog or pet on a leash: a shackle, fetter, or some other hobble device.

Just as importantly, here and now, the dog wears a special outfit, as a death row dog, as if a memorial for brothers and sisters, at one animal rescue center after another, and trapped in a typical cage, as if a savage, and that systemic erosion of civil liberties, of reasonable, of a subtle spirit on the rise, a John Locke notion of liberty, or some other cultural equivalent; of hope, a universal freedom, an ever so smooth phase transition, where the conscious gradually unfolds, as a legato complex, or evolution of a blank verse.

***

In addition, here and now, one crowd member after another leans toward the dog, to view from the front view, side, then back.

***

And on occasion, a person lightly pats the dog, especially a little lady, a five-year-old, Jennifer Congrego, from Houston, who wears her best floral Sunday dress mid-week, white socks with cute ruffle trim, and black patent leather shoes, of which projects an image of a "true young lady" in all respects, and no one should doubt, especially the parents.

So much so, she pats and pats then looks deeply into the dog eye with full compassion, respect, and youthful glow; as if true satisfaction, such as *santosha, samayach, eudaimonia,* then bliss.

***

Of which, the dog notices, then fully appreciates civility.

And at that sight, one person after another glows happiness, becomes a luminaire, quintessence.

***

Yet a nearby person grumbles, "What the hell?"

And says ever so crudely, "What kind of dog is this?" as if a professional grump, such as a glum, grump, frump and mugwump.

A person well known for a poverty of ideas.

Or, said as if in a classic top-down regimental style system, a rut; that often makes matters worse, as a crude plow through complex material, and a regimental style that concentrates tremendous power into a deep rut, feudalism.

CHAPTER 11

▼

PART 2

Then one crowd member after another recalls yesterday, at the same time, the dog was dressed as a bunny rabbit, with cute fluffy ears, as if truly civilized, and quite self-aware.

CHAPTER 11

▼

PART 3

And the day before, it dressed as a cat, *Felis silvestris catus* or *Felis catus*, *Felidae*, an Oligocene, and that belief system.

***

Yet, the dog did so not as an "oppositional defiant disorder," and with no intent to mock the Felidae system, spirit, and each aspiration, each breath; each loud breathing sound, as a result of air passing thru an abnormally narrowed passageways, meeting resistance to airflow; that cranial system, of partial blockage of regions.

***

As, this dog appeared to do so, with respectful homage, yet as a reasonable spoof, a light humorous parody, to vent tension, physics, universal law.

CHAPTER 11

▼

PART 4

And to some New York crowd members, the dog seems, well; it seems, ever so cool, especially for a dog that appears culturally "up to speed," real time, and based on one topic of decency after another.

***

And, as this dog moves thru the growing crowd towards, a fallen *Erika Segersäll Unræd*, the Scandinavian, things shift; and a closer inspection of this dog reveals a white muzzle, white cheeks, and typical wolf markings.

Yet this dog seems as if a proto-dog, a prehistoric wolf dog, or *Canis chihliensis, Epicyon haydeni*, yet as if somehow, it is the mother of all the wolf and dog species, such as the evolutionary origin of both and prehuman empire, an *ab initio*?

And in this case, it seems quite unique.

In addition, this Manhattan dog appears ever so alert, yet not easily ruffled, and more than willing to learn, such as with one excellent inborn cue management skill after another.

So much so, it has an exceptional bearing, and seems truly civilized, as if the origin or supplement of every known stable civilization, and variations of, an *ab initio*?

Such as, pre-human civilization needed a little something else, something extra, for example, a companion, proxy, stabilizing agent, and frontier guide with another perspective and practical skills to supplement human limitations and bias, and not more of the same-old, same-old human tendencies that develop over time, a vast collection of things, including words yet an exceptionally poor ability to communicate with other humans and their animal neighbors.

***

Yet from another angle, this dog resembles a *Jämthund*, Swedish Elkhound/Moose hound, a Spitz from Northern Europe, based on mitochondrial DNA subclade; a female wolf and domestic male dog hybrid.

However, from a different angle, this dog resembles a Norwegian *Buhund* then moments later, Finnish Spitz, a dynamic lively, curious, intelligent, independent and brave dog, with exceptionally fine hearing. And a loyal service breed, a devoted, true all-around canine known for an ability to effectively explore the frontier, such as one remote frontier Scandinavian trail after another, and one complex rocky situation after another, such as one precarious highland maneuver after another, and up a considerable cliff, with precarious foot placement that often crumbles, a crumble accumulate potential in various locations; and of greater importance, a call to action, a call to an adventure, and destiny in the Big Show, monomyth cycle, and truly great threshold adventure into the majestic.

CHAPTER 11

▼

PART 5

Here and now, this dog seems ever so calm, confident, composed, and with a complex self-assured personality; not easily ruffled, as if a steady partner ever-so-true, such as at home, or in the great frontier, and as if an all-around canine partner, tracker, hunter, guardian, herder, and tenacious defender known for courage, and true grit.

CHAPTER 12

▼

THE SPARROW

Moments later, in the Manhattan clear blue expanse of sky, not far from that accident, an ever so tiny bird rapidly approaches this accident; a sparrow, and with one considerable technique after another, of short flapping "bursts" that alternate, with an interval, where wings tightly fold against the body, a "bounding" technique, or "flap-bounding" flight, yet primarily, as if a ballistic.

***

Or say another way in great depth, the sparrow "bounds" toward, as if a range function, or as a "number less than or equal to every number in a set."

Or say another way, the sparrow leaps thru the air, with one special transitional technique after another, a series of spring inbound; a leap thru time and space, to cover a great distance, with one extraordinary "leap of faith" after another.

***

And eventually, as if a virtuoso, this tiny sparrow glides down, ever so smooth, close to the accident, to nearby "prominent" position, then perches.

***

Then, one at a time, in great detail, it carefully studies each significant crowd member.

***

And, for a better vantage point, it leaps closer, and closer.

Then once ever so certain, it lands on one exceptional Manhattan crowd member right shoulder after another, as if to confer, and often, in the ear, discreetly chirps a message.

***

And on occasion, it leaps, and lands on a poorly disguised crowd member, who minor reels on contact, such as poker, know those skills, especially self-control, for example, suppress each body expressions, yet thoughts remain highly active, as if a real-time event.

***

So much so, and each time, as the sparrow lands, that person looks at one very specific crowd reference point after another, mostly focus on a personal trait or fashion trait, a reference cue, as if a cue management technique.

Then that person quietly shifts into an ever so serious look to the bird, of say nothing, such as "never ever," and of equal importance, try to maintain a poker face, as much of life has a poker game quality.

***

Moments later, the sparrow leaps then "glides," ever so smooth, into prime time live!

CHAPTER 13

▼

PART 1

A NOBEL COMMITTEE MEMBER, SWEDISH ACADEMY COMMITTEE SECRETARY, AND PERMANENT SEASONED ADVISER

Then, the bird lands on a windowsill, at eye level, in front of three people.

And eventually, then ever so carefully, the tiny sparrow hops closer to these three people, and studies them thru social, personal, then intimate space, as if proxemics, an avian version of, how to study human use of space and those effects, for example haptic, kinesic, vocalic, chronemic, the structure of time, and other constructs mostly hidden.

And the sparrow continues to carefully study each person, especially body language, clothing, mood, then compares to last month, at the edge of one Norwegian meeting after another, those patterns; as if each and every cue offers more and more insight of humans.

***

So much so, here and now, the sparrow studies these three people, a Norwegian Nobel Committee member, new Swedish Academy committee secretary, and permanent seasoned adviser-well known in Scandinavia as "the specialist," a cultural linguistic specialist, often called upon for knowledge about specific candidate skill sets, clarity, efficiency, effectiveness, realism and ability to reveal nature.

An advisor, who normally lives near one of Oslo's golden ghettos for the elite, Oslo's West Side, a dense concentration of people with exceptionally large bank accounts, and in this case *Bygdøy allé*.

And, this advisor is often called upon as an expert judge of "Talent and Taste," of "*Snille och Smak*," the primary purpose of that Academy, to further the purity, strength, and fully reveal the aesthetics of nature, the universe, to explore one branch after another, such as science, art, beauty, taste, and especially the sublime features of the Swedish language, and indirectly Northern Scandinavian languages of Uralic, Finno-Ugric and Samoyedic, of Northern Eurasia, and language in general, such as the ability to accurately communicate.

Or say another way, the advisor searches for a well-crafted mastery of language, the ways and means to communicate and reveal a culture, especially the practical and aesthetics of science, art, beauty, and the sublime, to reveal one mystery of existence after another, and often, what appears as if an untranslatable idea, character, function, setting, or system, of something "beyond all language and thought, and beyond all categories of being, is it, or is it not?"

***

Or say another way, the ways and means to free a nation, the ultimate prize, to recover and improve the culture, into the best version of a truly great society.

And, this advisor is an expert judge of descriptive abilities, such as fully explore any given setting, event, character, family, tribe, culture, diaspora, and swirl of ideas.

Then judge if, the work offers a compelling story, and/or, a "high concept" page turning adventure, with a profound thematic structure.

And, do these characters, ideas, settings and events have depth, then one compelling perspective or angle after another.

And, do things evolve, and eventually mature?

Does the work explore one relationship after another, and at any given moment, in great depth, such as to study a people, organization, place, condition, time, sequence, and purpose, cause, effect, results, and show historical context, such as to the human species, a history of?

***

And, does the work have proper spelling?

And equally important, does it communicate in a clear, organized, concise, accurate, grammatically correct, and persuasive manner, and, on occasion, with an extraordinary style, elegance, and charm, to reveal true human potential, such as an ability to seamlessly flow, as if a virtuoso, with a certain flow, rhythm, style, and *panache*, especially in a classic problematic situation of people, a spiral of silence, cycle of poverty, *Vicious Circle* by Jacek Malczewski, self-fulfilling prophecy, or a dense metaphorical forest filled with thorny brier extensions, of same-old, same-old, of life as a lowly trope or "redshirt," a disposable stock character.

And, does the story deploy a clever last-second literal or metaphorical sidestep maneuver, or more, then plow, then hard right, plow, hard left, plow, and one spin maneuver after another to untangle.

Then battle towards a metaphorical forest exit, to a clear line of freedom, of free at last.

And eventually find a considerable sense of tranquility, as if a restoration; that could generate a-wellbeing-on-the-rise, then one spark, crackle, and thought after another; about a clean escape; about the artistry of guile, grit, and true determination, and a bit of luck, fate, karma and/or randomness of nature; and about the sheer delight, of one new opportunity after another.

That now seems possible—a new world, a new place bright, fresh, free, and fair; and one that contains beauty and poetic landscape; such as a neo-romance aesthetic.

That includes improved Platonic notions of beauty, spirit, freedom, and the full potential of individual creativity, aspiration, and opportunity.

For example, a place that leads beyond the fundamental threshold, and all those very particular expressions, compelling degrees of transcendence; into a full restoration of lost glory?

***

Does the work show any of these traits, and a certain refined sense of judgment, sentiment and taste; as a scholarship, to advance culture, civilization, the human species?

***

Or, of greater importance, does the work reveal an amateur in search of a fast buck, a trope, a flimflam, or, common swindler with a simple linguistic trick or scheme, or from obsessively tinkering with things, with tricks that ignore the fundamental rules of nature, system, symmetry, symbiosis, "set and setting"; as if what happens when someone trips—really trips—trips into a theater of the truly absurd?

***

And, does the literary work convey obvious and nuanced meanings; often quite subtle, yet accurate; and use one appropriate communication style after another?

Such as, situationally fitted with an appropriate rhetorical device or technique; of "virtual salt"; and how both best function, as a sapient, prudent, shrewd management of practical affairs; as a prudent investor of vital circumspection, piquancy and permanence, of which helps regulate engaging provocative charm, and the lively arch charm device of "wit," to reach beyond a quagmire, of same-old, same-old, of life as a trope.

***

And, does the work have "fundamental" characters in every sense of the word, such as configured with paired opposites, dynamics, companions and dependents, to more fully reveal the human condition, in one setting after another?

And, does the work evoke prime time live, where anything is possible, and anyone one can take over the storyline?

▼

PART 2

Or, does the work evoke something else, something?

▼

PART 3

In a serious way, does the work promote freedom?

Or if need be, silly, such as the ability to spontaneously express freedom, real freedom, to explore life thru literature, and maybe later, if need be, for relief, with a dance, the best of "Harlem shake!"

CHAPTER 14

▼

Intermission

CHAPTER 15

▼

A PROPER GREETING?

Moments later, near that Manhattan accident, and to one person at a time, in the proper sequence, first with the Norwegian Nobel Committee member, new Swedish Academy committee secretary, and permanent seasoned adviser well known in Scandinavia as "the specialist," the sparrow chirps an ever so polite greeting, in fact quite charming, and does so in full accord with the classic greeting protocol, as a protocol suite of one exceptional courtesy after another.

Or say another way, the tiny bird does so with a protocol-relative URL; of how to approach and the address "bar," and bar in every known definition, such as approach, do so as "proper art," a well-known player yet ever so humble, such as Andy Player of Rosa, or some other appropriate cultural equivalent spirit.

***

However, and each time, with each proper sparrow chirp protocol routine, these three people minor reel.

***

And, the sparrow finds this quite odd.

So much so, the bird minor finches here and there, as if to gain one better angle after another, as if an index, an econometric index by time series, of the long game.

Or put another way, a differential game, such as the continuous pursuit and evasion, and the play of one game develops the rules for another game.

Or put a third way, the bird searches for details, mission, function, timing, and so forth, such as the ultimate insider strategy guide, a "first mover advantage effort," a short or long game.

And again, none of these people seem fixated or obsessed, as the eyes appear normal, and not cold, barren of empathy, such as stuck on the last war or two, stuck in history, in an aspect of a trouble tree, niche, or bubble, and that crude form of escalation, the bandwagon effect, to bang the drum!

CHAPTER 16

▼

And to the sparrow, all seems a bit odd, as these people know it quite well, have introduced themselves many times in Scandinavia, in fact, hand-fed it ever so tasty snacks, wonderful crispy morsels.

And often, to it, baby-talked, made ogle noises, those classic "goo-goo gaa-gaa" baby talk sounds, to charm her, as well as showed her those faces, those exaggerations baby girls receive, those, "Oh, so pretty.

"She is such a wonderful darling!"

And, "She's so cute!"

"And, how did you get so cute?

"Come on.

"Tell me, how did you get so cute?"

Yet today, these people maintain a poker face, and seem as if in denial, especially of common courtesy, or something else; as humans often seem trapped in a niche, a special mental dimension, of linear thought yet loop, an elaborate construct, or yet another contract, often a read-ahead loop yet historical quagmire, or the big data dilemma, based on the telencephalon expanse, as compared to the diencephalon, medulla, or other bases, to measure each and every reference cues.

***

In fact, these three people only minor reel with each polite greeting.

So, the tiny bird attempts to charm them, quite so.

And, it chirps a universal melody, as if a melody master, with a tune yet line, that seems as if a single entity, of one musical phrase and motif after another throughout the song, then sings the "oldest known melody," as if ever so true, charmed spirit, yet cosmopolitan and ever so genteel, such as a cultured being on the rise.

CHAPTER 17

▼

And yet, these three people maintain a poker face.

So much so, the bird carefully looks about, seriously considers one thing after another, pauses for a few seconds, mentally sparks, then chirps with an unusual technique, for something.

***

And moments later, that dog, or whatever it is, a proto-dog, a prehistoric wolf dog, or *Canis chihliensis, Epicyon haydeni* hears, perks, knows very well, carefully looks about, then quietly barks a complex phrase to that pet duck, on a leash that could easily break, as the leash appears symbolic, a prophetic, an adaptive regression or additive contemplative technique.

So much so, the duck straightens posture, carefully looks about, quacks a reply, then an unusual message, to any person that shows an interest, as it plows thru the Manhattan crowd, that, for the most part, step to one side or the other, and stare, really stare at this odd site, of an unusual dog, that walks a strange pet duck, well ahead on leash, as if the duck has a considerable number of "rights," and defined as if all definitions of the word based on Middle English, from Old English *riht,* a mistranslation?

***

However, here and now, on occasion a stubborn "grump" stands proudly in the way, and bellows this and that, mostly about me-me-me, it's all about me.

Such as, the type of person, if placed in paradise, would poke and poke, or fiddle with it, and fiddle, or pick at it, and really pry at it with an idea, law, process, construct, or pry with a crowbar—where a thing might stand for 1,000 years or more as is, yet, people, and nature, especially a grump, or nature itself pries, with various techniques, such as a rhizome wedge.

Or say another way, a glum, grump, gripe, or glum, grump, frump, mugwump, a loud irritable person blocks the duck's path.

***

Of which, the duck carefully looks about this situation, one nearby significant crowd member after another, then especially that person from head to toe, as if they have a poverty of ideas and thoughts, a systematic "rut" blocks the path, based on Middle English *rutte*, a major disturbance, a defiant disorder, an oppositional defiant disorder (ODD), DSM-5, a pattern of, one irritable mood after another, quick to anger, argumentative that lacks logic, and true peer reviewable facts, then shows one defiant behavior after another, that seriously implies a truly vindictive being?

***

And that irritable person, who blocks the duck and dog path, rants on and on about "the Manhattan public leash law," which "requires a dog or other pet on a leash": a shackle, fetter, or some other hobble device.

And, this person wildly gestures, then rants on and on about one pet outfit after another, especially as the dog wears a death row dog outfit, as if a memorial for brothers and sisters, at one animal rescue center after another, and trapped in a typical cage, as if a savage; and that systemic erosion of civil liberties, of reasonable, of a subtle spirit on the rise, a John Locke notion of liberty, or some other cultural equivalent; of hope, a universal, of freedom, an ever so smooth phase transition, where the conscious and spirit gradually unfolds, an evolution, a legato, blank verse, or metrical, and rise oh noble spirit, rise, rise!

***

Of which, the dog and duck respectfully listen, to one loud gesticulate rant philosophy after another, and mostly formulated with a heuristic bias, then another, often with mixed metaphors, at least to nearby crowd members.

***

Yet, in their own way, the pets think ahead, and only hear "blah-blah-blah," typical human gibber gabber, of one obsessive construct after another, to reinvent something for the umpteenth time, and now sold emphatically as the one true irritable path, or face destruction, a favorite human hobby, give a stark choice, barren of three dimensions, reasonable context, and content.

As a result, humans often prefer some equivalent of stepping on something, maybe an idea, philosophy, system, or ant, and really mash and mash it into the ground, into nothing, as if out of history.

***

Then respectfully, here and now, the pets seriously consider the grumpy demands, shrug what, look about, shrug what again, has seen this show before, the theme, and instead plow pass, one loud Manhattan gesticulate ranting grump after another, as these pets have no interest in a prison oubliette, epiphanic or cardboard, to restrict degrees of freedom.

***

And eventually, the duck and dog arrive at the sparrow and those three people, a Norwegian Nobel Committee member, Swedish Academy committee secretary, and permanent seasoned adviser well known in Scandinavia as "the specialist," a cultural linguistic specialist, often called upon for knowledge about specific candidate skill sets, clarity, efficiency, effectiveness, realism and ability to reveal nature.

And of course, in the proper order, one at a time, the duck offers each of the four, an ever so polite avian greeting, in fact quite charming, and does so in full accord with the classic greeting protocol, as a protocol suite of one exceptional courtesy after another, a protocol-relative URL; of how to approach and the address "bar," and bar in every known definition, with a proper ever so subtle variation of "quack, quack, quack," other sounds and appropriate body language.

Then the dog speaks its version, with ever so subtle onomatopoeia manner and style of mumbles, barks, woofs, hisses, and other sounds with an unexplained accent that seem quite articulate for a dog, especially if a person listens, truly listens, yet nearly every human would not, and treat it as odd nonsense, quite, or a cute trick.

However, during this greeting, and on occasion, the dog also uses a subtle paw sign language on the ground, of paw spelling shorthand, and other gestures, yet not mudras, as paws are unable to offer those complex abilities.

And the greeting shows of how a sentence grows, cumulative syntax to create degrees of suspense, and the mechanics-of-delay, as if a master sentence yet from a canine viewpoint?

***

And oddly enough, in totality, this elaborate canine greeting conveys figurative and metaphorical traits, of connotation and innuendo, such as sign, speech, and action that suggest certain meanings, ideas, concepts, systems and so on, of which suggest a metaphysical poet trying to convey what is quite difficult to express in words, the unexplainable, or what is beyond all language and thought, and effort to describe a great mystery, an unknown; yet get as close to as possible, to the great frontier, with a canine *pathopoeia* language?

***

Yet, something seems a bit off, as if words and phrases from the canine version of The *Devil's Dictionary*, often a witty unique perspective and one insult after another, often a play on words; in short, a smart aleck that makes comments in one clever way after another, to poke fun at human traits or combinations of, obsessive, petty, supercilious, and thugs, for principal sake, whether rich or poor?

***

However, none of those three people or nearby crowd members understand any of this dogspeak, dog linguistic style, techniques, grammar, literal and figurative references.

Similar to, people cannot understand a gorilla, such as Hanabiko, Koko, July 4, 1971-June 19, 2018, a female western lowland gorilla, or...

57

..., mostly, a misunderstood being, especially the sounds, sound symbolism, speech, mimicry, gestures, the gestics, timing, temporal inflection, of content, context, acclimation, phenotypic plasticity, then, introduce a major species adjustment, yet treated as quite minor, as a circus act, as yet another disposable, a history of the human species, quite dismissive, of a true meritocracy.

**

Yet, here and now, that Scandinavian expert, quickly notices a canine meaning here and there, especially the linguistic subtly, nevertheless says nothing, and maintains a poker face.

**

As most systems expect full compliance with their belief system, such as obey or else.

And, no one in their right mind would say dogs or other animals could talk, could communicate in an articulate way; that reveals one higher order thinking skill after another, and metacognition, "thinking about thinking," "knowing about knowing," and self-awareness, introspection, propositional attitudes, deliberate individualizationable skills, *qualia*, unique canine philosophy of the mind, clever wit, a real smart aleck, a troublemaker, the type parents and authorities warn, "Stay away from those people, ideas, concepts, systems, or whatever."

***

And, if a person says so, says dogs are articulate, then likely, the person would be labeled as foolish, then quickly discredited, and labeled a dupe, and/or a deranged person; a person who deserves a slight, for example treated with private and especially public contempt; and outed by a person who acts as if, yet another impulse wantabe, a town crier.

***

Again, maybe this dog's communication is all nonsense, a trick, mimic, rote memory, such as Koko the gorilla, and other well-known pets?

***

And, because of no interest whatsoever, to acknowledge these pet greetings, the duck, tiny sparrow, and dog puzzle among each other, and again, then seriously confer.

So much so, the pets chat for some time then vote, with a right wing, left wing, and right back paw.

Yet the duck and sparrow are not amused, not at all.

So, the dog sobers, offers the best front paw vote, and the birds nod thanks, then the sparrow turns to the Nobel trio and sings a vital question.

***

As a result, it truly startles the Nobel trio, as it implies a universal question, a sense–denotation distinction, of "When will the golden age arrive?

***

Such as, the human equivalent of, "When will I arrive in the garden paradise, a perennial Neoplatonism, a shared metaphysical truth yet origin in full accord with the Bhagavad Gita, and other cradles of civilizations, where they meet, they converge and share a universal truth?

Or say another way, by a mathematical geek, "Share a universal, a property category theory, such as of free people and objects, in a truly great garden paradise."

Or say another way, by a mathematical geek, "When will the golden age arrive of variety, universal algebra, seamless physical system functions and garden structures that seem infinite, mostly unseen, in full accord with all members."

***

And all the while, as this sparrow sings a question to the human trio, the Nobel trio try to maintain a poker face.

Yet on occasion, that specialist seems unable to hide an understanding, of bits here and there, then quietly shifts into an ever so serious look of: say nothing, such as "never ever," and of equal importance, try to maintain a poker face, as much of life has a poker game quality.

Because most systems expect full compliance with their belief system, such as obey or else.

And no one in their right mind would say dogs or animals could talk, could communicate, especially in an articulate way.

And if a person said so, they would likely be labeled a fool or insane then quickly discredited, often unemployed, and/or squished with metaphorical leather shoe or muddy combat boot, as if a bug; really squished.

In addition, an investigator should maintain a semblance of neutrality, of impartiality.

***

Yet today, the Nobel trio seem, as if above it all, and refuse to recognize a traditional or elaborate greeting, or that universal question.

So much so, it has delayed the pet mission, the main reason for this visit, to offer an update on *Erika Segersäll Unræd*, the Scandinavian.

CHAPTER 18

▼

PART 1

Eventually, and one at a time, the pet sparrow, dog, and duck try to, in their own way, meticulously explain the overall situation, especially about the accident.

***

And often, the sparrow offers one gesture after another, such as visible nonverbal bodily actions, to communicate a series of very particular messages, as it offers a complex combination of "clicks, chirps, chinks, cheeps, chirrups, seeps, squawks" and other noises, then one song after another with the descriptive expressivity of an advance intricate whistled language, that shocks a few nearby people.

***

Or say another way, a high whistled speech, it emulates, makes an equivalent of one tone and vowel after another that natural spoken language has, to create a compressed yet "articulate efficient functional load," of which is no small accomplishment, such as convey intonation, prosody-suprasegmental-suprasegmentally, and one linguistic unit after another, to show precise intense mental activity, of mood, temperament, personality, disposition, and motivation, and quite certain degrees of pleasure or displeasure, on one subject after another, and yet as if a genesis of a major whistled language.

***

Although, many of the human onlookers, see and hear, yet think, all these sounds seem as if odd nonsense, quite, especially as after, the dog tries to communicate with a subtle onomatopoeia manner, and style of complex combinations of mumbles, barks, subtle woofs, reasonable hisses, other sounds, and with an unexplained Scandinavian accent, if a person listens, truly listens.

Yet nearly everyone does not, and treats it as odd, maybe nonsense, or a trick.

***

And during, on the ground, the dog uses one subtle paw sign language after another, of paw spelling, yet especially shorthand, as Koko the gorilla often created a more natural variation of human language, or gorillas, or universal, or one better species adapted for both canines and avians.

Or say in technical terms, a combinatoric, a run-time theoretical classification, often of estimates that anticipate shortcomings of language and empirical metrics, the problematics of "upper bound linguistic performance," often a max-q substitute, or sample scenario.

***

Yet here and now, for the most part one person after another mumbles, "Odd nonsense."

"Strange."

Or, "No way."

As a result, the dog and birds realize, puzzle among themselves, then quietly confer, as if this is not the golden age of humans, sapiens, yet a civilization that believes in an enemy-of-the-month club, to earn a living, and that chain of events.

CHAPTER 18

▼

PART 2

And to the pets, yes-yes-yes, these people have plenty of stuff, such as things, interesting devices, manner of dress, speech, food, especially crispy bacon, yet often, a substitute, mostly artificial, such as a path into yet another quagmire.

And social systems in general, often mandate a collar, harness, or contract, whether literal or metaphorical, to tie down a creature and/or person, and for one reason or another, often as a modern servant or various categories of wage slave, and often as a vivid wayward lesson, and sometimes treat as Gordon, aka, Whipped Peter, or some other cultural equivalent?

***

And mandate, not able to walk free from the foundation, the system, free from trafficking, commercial exploitation, psychological coercion of obey and sit.

For example, often considered as if property, often from birth, or a simple mistake or contract, to be bought and rented as a common animal, a beast of burden, a pack animal.

Or often, on command, fetch and serve a stick, or idea, memory, emotion, mood, temperament, personality, disposition, philosophy, tradition, system, yet often a quandary.

***

And often, commanded to do so as if bait.

So, go-go-go, yet do not look behind the curtain, and fetch then serve a stick or equivalent, for substandard water, sugary treat, starch, and/or crisp bacon; or more likely, for a crude commercial trick, ingredients, or *antefix*, a concealing technique, and ends that join sections of humanity, that precarious edge of artificially constructed crumble, a history of the human species?

CHAPTER 19

▼

Yet, and one at a time, the Norwegian Nobel Committee member, Swedish Academy committee secretary, and permanent seasoned adviser well known in Scandinavia as "the specialist" notice in the air, sniff, and again, then at one angle after another, and find a potent spirit on the rise.

***

And the Swedish Academy committee secretary's face changes, to alert, interest, keen, anticipation, absorbed, engrossed, then as if a secular mystery, a vision, and then, into an ever so peaceful poetic *aristo* daydream, a natural language, a natural flow of speech and grammatical units, one after another, and vivid substantial structure, and as if to conjure something, something; and to charge with one impressive solemn and earnest thought degree after another.

Such as, if to summon, invoke, an incantation, then filled with one image after another, to "conjure up, a metaphorical, biochemical, and/or hidden dark matter biome need, or needs" or, a R. J. Kaufmann idea, yet done so as if *Eyvindr Finnsson skáldaspillir*, skaldic verse, runic inscription, or *Rök* Runestone, or some other cultural equivalent.

***

Then ever so groggy, the Swedish Academy committee secretary slowly mumbles; yet gradually becomes quite clear, and often pauses at the end of each deliberate phrase, when commenting about the air, that smell, and again, of a potent spirit on the rise.

And, this committee secretary slowly says, as if found, "An educated sustenance, yes, a masterpiece, a single special batch, and with sufficient pure spirit, in each simple distillation "stage," in every sense of the word, to make a cleaner, an ever so lighter spirit, of two-wash, four spirits, from wash, feint, spirit, *fore* shot, *dud run, wee witchee,* and the heart process."

So much so, the Norwegian Nobel Committee member and permanent seasoned adviser, well known in Scandinavia as "the specialist" turns towards the Swedish Academy committee secretary, as if, about this person, they now have a major revelation; they now know so much more about this person, who normally remains stern, yet proper, quite distant, aloof, as if a mystery.

***

And, much to their surprise, the Swedish Academy committee secretary continues ever so discreet, subtle, and serious, "Yes-yes-yes, this dog sipped an exceptional 100-year-old whiskey, a previous nip, or two?

***

And the Swedish Academy committee secretary eyes narrow, as he says, "Yes," and carefully look about for a plenipotentiary, stateless elite, Davos, or a wealthy secular hermit.

***

Then, the secretary eyes narrow, and carefully looks for a potential Westphalian sovereign, a Manhattan exceptional, yet says nothing.

So much so, and eventually, the Norwegian Nobel Committee member, with an ever so serious look at the secretary, yet self-restrains, minor reels to one angle after another, as if to carefully measure each and every mysterious secretary action, then turns toward the specialist, leans ever so close and quietly mumbles, "Really?

"Interesting."

And the specialist says, "Quite."

Then, the Swedish Academy committee secretary motions the dog closer.

And, it inches forward, a bit.

Yet say, as if skepticism, and a considerable interest, "No...!

"Closer."

***

And, with great detail, the dog looks at one vital crowd member after another, as if searching for something or someone, an ultimate insider, and another, yet eventually, and reluctantly, the dog edges a bit closer.

Then, the Swedish Academy committee secretary softly says, "No, no, no.

"Closer."

And, it does, bit by bit.

Yet the duck notices something else, and really stares.

***

Then, it quacks a complex phrase to the dog, who nods in complete agreement.

Then the duck, in a different direction, plows thru the dense crowd, and plows, then arrives at a poor disguised person, a great pretender, who discreetly shakes a head, and mumbles as if to hide, "Go away."

It does not.

"Go away."

It does not, and seriously looks into this person's eyes, then politely chatters a greeting.

"I'm serious.

"Go away."

It does not, then asks avian style, a vital question.

Then, after no reply, it quickly summaries the event and storyline.

Then, this poor disguised person says ever so soft and discreetly, "Pretend you don't know me.

"Please.

"Please?"

It does not.

Then as if asking for true mercy, "Please."

***

As a result, the duck notices something elsewhere, well beyond, and again, nods yes to the great pretender, then in different direction, it plows pass one grump after another, that notices it and shakes a mighty fist to the 955th, of the known heavens, then says one truly filthy curse after another, words quite profane, and not fit for print.

***

***

And a reader may notice, that much of the above section has been removed, as a young reader may receive a true shock.

And enough so, that the young reader may also put two and two together, such as things previously heard, sly phrases, overheard adult conversations, and other things often withheld from kids and young adults…

… to shield them from true human nature, the history of, from the behind-the-scene system…

… to shield from the ways and means, of so-called civilization, of how it really functions…

… as the word "civilization" could now take on a whole new meaning, such as the opposite, of crude, vulgar, and oppressive.

And "do as I say, not as I do," those double standards and much-much more, such as classic major, average and minor civilization exceptions, often a deliberate withholding vital facts and support, of misleading or lies said "special privileges of power," and a very selective memory, use of logic, facts, and history, the foundation, much of the human species?

***

And, as the duck plows thru the crowd, one grump after another yells at it, as if a true cuss master with one well-crafted foul saying and gesture after another, such as the bold cuss master tradition among military commanders.

Of which, a side note, many military services have a trash talking cuss tradition, and often based on everyday foul mouth themes.

And some of these tough military cuss masters are virtuosos, that thrive, and others deploy a high cultural style within this lowbrow art form. Think of it as a sweet science of exceptional foul-speak, designed to shock and provoke the senses.

And yet when done in an exceptionally well-crafted way, it can reveal a well-seasoned mind, as a sapient, prudent, shrewd, circumspect, piquant and engaging arch charm device of a stinging wit, that has a certain refined judgment, sentiment and taste, even scholarship—as odd as that sounds— with a well-crafted mastery of aesthetics, of nature, art, beauty, taste, and especially the sublime.

Offshoots exist.

And most have a longstanding tradition, yet in contrast to a warrior poet, of someone tough and courageous in battle, and yet has a certain cultured bearing, refinement, and well-seasoned agile mind.

And a warrior polymath, *polyhistor*, multipotentiality, comparative advantage, microeconomic theories, and/or renaissance poet, more than capable of delivering a fistic lesson.

Or, deliver a spinning karate chop to the throat, and again, and again.

Or, reveal some extraordinary scholastic insight, then contemplate the big questions of life and the universe, such as an unsolved problem in physics, mathematics, biology, medicine, chemistry, especially supramolecular chemistry, molecular self-assembly, molecular folding, molecular recognition, or music theory rhythm, bundle theory, melody, structure, form, texture, especially harmonics, as opposed to a common thug, savage, and barbarian.

***

Here and now, as this duck, that plows thru this crowd, it passes a woman, a relatively young, retired Arleigh Burke-class guided missile destroyer naval commander.

CHAPTER 20

▼

Meanwhile, the Norwegian Nobel Committee member, with an ever so serious look, motions the dog closer.

And, it inches a bit forward.

"No, closer."

And reluctantly, the dog carefully examines one crowd member after another, as if searching for something or someone, then the dog edges a bit closer.

"No, no, no, closer."

And the dog edges a bit closer.

"No, no, no, closer."

▼

PART 1

A COMMERCIAL BREAK

Consider something, other than Jools Holland and David Gray, "I Think It's Going to Rain Today"?

CHAPTER 22

▼

"Two, three, four!"

CHAPTER 23

▼

Then moments later, as the Norwegian Nobel Committee member reaches for and reads the dog's collar tag, elsewhere with due diligence, the duck plows thru this dense Manhattan crowd towards the accident.

***

And meanwhile, the committee member continues to read, reels a considerable amount, carefully looks about at the crowd, then dog in great detail, one angle after another, and back to the tag that says *MY NAME IS DOG. YES, SIMPLY CALL ME DOG, AND SAY IT WITH WILD EYES, EXAGGERATED GUSTO, OR SAY IT WITH HANDS EXTENDED OUT, PALMS UP TOWARDS THE HEAVENS, AND HANDS AS IF CLAWS, THEN SHAKE THEM WITH REAL STYLE.*

OR, SAY IN A VERY LOUD VOICE, AS IF YOU'RE A MISSION COMMANDER, SUCH AS TO KICK ASS, OR PUT ANOTHER WAY, IF YOU'RE IN A MOOD TO KICK ASS AND TAKE NAMES!

As a result, the member minor recoils, improves posture, and says, "Really? "Interesting."

And the committee member turns towards, the Swedish Academy committee secretary and permanent seasoned adviser, well known in Scandinavia as "the specialist," and says "I think this dog, especially the owner, are troublemakers, real troublemakers."

***

And the committee member says, yet often pauses after each phrase, as eyes narrow, looks about the dense crowd, then to the Swedish Academy committee secretary and permanent seasoned adviser, "Yes, a provocateur, or equivalent, especially as it directly relates to Westphalian sovereignty system, an agreement that respects principle of territorial integrity, the principles of international law that each nation-state maintains sovereignty over its territory, and domestic affairs, to the exclusion of all external powers, and especially on the principle of noninterference in another country's domestic affairs."

***

Again, the air around this dog, the committee member notices, that smell, a potent spirit on the rise.

***

"Yes," then often pauses after each phrase, that resembles a spell, to conjure a daydream venture, as eyes narrow, "This dog has been drinking whiskey, drinking an exceptionally educated sustenance, yes, a masterpiece, a single malt special, and with sufficient pure spirit, from each simple distillation 'stage,' in every sense of the word, to make a cleaner, an ever so lighter spirit, of two-wash, four spirits, from wash, feint, spirit, fore shot, dud run, wee witchee, and the heart."

***

And again, much to the Swedish Academy committee secretary's and permanent seasoned adviser's surprise, the committee member continues an ever so discreet, subtle, and serious, "Yes-yes-yes, this dog sipped an exceptional 100-year-old-or-more whiskey, a previous nip, or two."

***

And, what dog owner offers, or permits their pet dog, to drink extraordinarily expensive liquor, booze for breakfast, a plenipotentiary, stateless elite, Davos, or a wealthy secular hermit?

***

As a result, the committee member considers, then daydreams, as if a serious secular mystery.

CHAPTER 24

▼

Elsewhere, in the middle of that dense Manhattan morning rush-hour-crowd accident, David and *Erika Segersäll Unræd*, the Scandinavian, appear dead, quite.

And, as many crowd members jostle closer, the masses resists.

***

Yet a nurse named Mary, whose formal name is Maryport Shelby Segedunum, born under a willow tree, next to a stone wall, quickly yet respectfully elbows her way thru, with one smooth maneuver after another, and eventually, into a lifesaving position, to check for signs of life, the pulse, blood pressure, respiratory rate, body temperature, and any other signs of life.

***

And, it seems best to describe her as a "hello nurse," a natural brunette bombshell, who recently received a doctorate degree in nursing.

And, everything about her screams "Schwiiinnng!" as in stunning to the nth degree, a classic beauty.

So much so, this appearance causes a considerable number of men and women an initial jolt, to their senses, of which unsettles them, quite so, in one distinct series of reactions after another.

***

Yet, her clothing, hairstyle, manner, and movement deliberately understate attractiveness, as if to disguise it with every possible trick, such as to systematically conceal any trace of wow.

***

And, most people have a first impression skillset, and some people, more than others.

Yet, she seems unable to fool that level of detection.

Likewise, in the past, her clothing and hairstyle methods consistently seem off.

So much so, and in a way that seems quite frumpy, shabby, especially here and now, with a distinct lack of skill that ultimately translates again, into yet another signature look.

***

And strangely enough, after observing her for some time, something triggers within the observer, and it may connect to the adaptive unconscious, intuition, *déjà vu*, reason, or the mid soul, undersoul or oversoul, to the set, the universal container, or some combination.

Then each time, a series of mental events appear on the observer's face, of which resemble elaborate mental measurements, formulations, then moods transition from surprise, puzzle, engross, eager to move closer, hesitant, uneasy, cautious, then last-second resolution jolts to the same conclusion, as everyone goes out of the way to avoid mentioning this.

So much so, the end result generates a powerful distancing effect; even if a person stands in her personal space, and it creates an elephant-in-the-room effect.

Such as with Mary, the proxemics of interpersonal space seems quite different, within intimate, personal, social, and public space.

***

Or say another way, the ways and means that people relate to one another in space and time, the communicative codes of sight, sound, smell, touch, taste, thermal, other biometric cues, and proprioception, self-movement in relationship to others with each event sequence.

***

And, no one wants to mention this oddly complex phenomenon.

***

Then often, crowd members focus on her systematic efforts, to save this woman.

Yet, *Erika Segersäll Unræd*, the Scandinavian, appears dead.

CHAPTER 25

▼

And in this crowd, as if seriously irritated from yet another daily commute delay, another disruption, so move along, someone in a loud crass way says, "So, people die.

"It happens?

"Look.

"In fact, it happens all the time.

"No big deal," as if, an ever so crude-reoccurring thematic in society, especially nature, such as clip something out, a weed, or series of in a complex system, or clip a specie, or more.

So "Move along.

"People die.

"Things die."

***

Then moments later, something else happens, something.

***

And, in their own time, one crowd member after another turns toward this person, and stares, really stares.

***

And eventually, that person shrugs; as if *Erika* were a disposable, "It happens!" such as clip a tree branch, or clip the tree of life with no implications, none, and clip, and clip, or "roundup ready," or better yet, alternate both with that pattern?

And to some people, this instantly leaves a full impression of indifference, of cold-bloodedness, such when their time arrives, this type of person will walk on their grave and treat their life, a memory of, as a yet another insignificant, a meaningless life, then may joke, cackle and plan to "take everything that isn't nailed down, and if it is, check for loose nails or boards," that personality type, the obsessive, the "addict pattern," with the highest degree of denial at the core, an omnivore?

As if life has no dignity, no worth, honor, or esteem, no exalted rank.

***

And, said as if no respect for the precariousness of life, and the route it must take, such as that unbroken generational chain of events, one after another, that ultimately created *Erika*; whether a bible-thumping 10,000-year chain, or some other cultural version of *religio*.

Or, think of it another way, a secular four billion years or so unbroken generational chain of events that created *Erika*, such as the anatomically modern human, human predecessors, truly great ape, ape, primate, mammal, amphibian, bilaterian, animal, multicellular life, complex cell, simple cell, biogenic glop, then pre-organic gunk, also known as slop within a variation of Hades, within a hellish early conditions on Earth, of an extreme bombardment.

And that entire precarious unbroken chain, over time, led to the eventual creation of a childless *Erika*.

***

Of which, and again, that professional grump crowd member, shrugs off this event as trivial.

It happens all the time, and with many species, so shrug off this unique universal event, then another, another?

CHAPTER 26

▼

PART 1

And moments later, in that dense, early morning Manhattan crowd, an impeccably dressed doctor, refuses to wait, as ever so stubborn people continue to block here and there, with a typical New York gridlock; that seems everywhere, and after each adjustment.

✳✳✳

And, is there a proper way, to plow thru this crowd, or in general, any crowd?

Such as, is there a good technique, as if as a farmer in the field, or do so as the art of sailing, that uses indirect ways and means, with one tact after another, and adjust to a powerful wind and wave of resistance?

✳✳✳

So, with reasonable frustration, the doctor loudly says, "Excuse me.
"Pardon me.
"Yes, pardon me.
"I'm a doctor."
And that allows one ever so narrow squeeze thru after another.
"Thank you.
"Yes, thank you.

Then, the doctor accidentally bumps into someone, and again, "Oops, I didn't mean to touch you there—honestly.

"You seem nice.

"I was bumped, into you.

"Or wait, said another way, someone bumped me, into you," and the head motions back, towards an oversized man, a huge mountain of humanity, burly, fit, and one warm buttermilk biscuit under 300 pounds, as in a man with no neck, barrel chest, and massive back, a real he-man.

And quite likely, he closely shaved ninety minutes ago, yet now has considerable five o'clock shadow.

Then the impeccably dressed doctor quickly scans this massive man head to toe, for a brief impression, with the adaptive unconscious, that rapid and automatic mental process only needs a second or two.

And, it reveals a true classic in his own right, as this man wears an impeccably tailored suit made with the finest materials, and shoes that may have cost $3,000 or more, such as Tom Ford, Sutor Mantellassi, or Stemar.

As a result, this massive human offers a truly menacing glare, as eyes bulge and powerful square jaws clench, grinds, and grinds then growls, and again.

***

So much so, and with both hands, the doctor pats the air towards this massive human then says, "Whoa!

"Wait a minute, I ... I...," looks towards that accident, then mountain of humanity.

And that causes this massive person, to flash a glare, all of which comes across as quite menacing, especially as this person subtly motions elsewhere in the crowd, and another location, to similar men, real he-man.

***

And one after another, they notice, eyes widen, narrow, and alert, then discreetly whisper into a sleeve, of which activates what, a network, system, an empire, a modern epic narrative, an acculturation, set, setting, found to date, variation, a modern adaption of the Kurukshetra War thematics, of recurring salient motifs, a story about the fate of struggling dynastics, of too-big-to-fail, or some other cultural equivalent?

***

And dynastic powers that compete, in one form of ever so consuming conflict after another, that often relies on dreadful secret alliances, and "close enough"; in an ever so shallow language-game, a dereistic, then hyper metanarrative chase, of zoom-zoom-zoom; and the irony of a self-made trap, of yet another quagmire, or same-old, same-old; which causes any given system to lose one thing after another, such as truly great function, mission, voyage, depth, so many victims, such as children, elderly, heroes and heroines, yet a reoccurring theme in the human species, nature, and the universe?

***

Or say another way, another expensive shortcut, sold as low cost and effective, another metaheuristic, or a new version of *Ars Conjectandi*, as if yet another Machiavelli product theme, or some other construct sold as "the new normal"?

So much so, it may remind a person of something, maybe a familiar song lyric of, "When your love has moved away, you must face yourself and say"?

***

▼

PART 2

As a result, the impeccably dressed doctor turns to that bumped person and says, "Again, pardon me," then plows towards the accident, thru this crowd with one exceptional technique after another, as if the art of sailing, with one carefully measured tact after another.

***

And, the doctor says with a reasonable yet loud frustration, "Excuse me.
"Pardon me.
"Yes, pardon me.
"I'm a doctor."
And that allows, one ever so narrow squeeze thru after another.
"Thank you.
"Yes, thank you.

***

Then, the doctor bumps into someone, and again, "Oops, I didn't mean to touch you there—honestly."
And eventually, the impeccably dressed doctor arrives at the accident, scans the immediate area, the *mise en* scene, moves into a lifesaving position,

and checks for signs of life; the pulse, blood pressure, respiratory rate, body temperature, and any sign of life; searches for one pattern after another.

***

And, not far away, another impeccably dressed doctor plows thru the dense crowd, and arrives, and another, as if Manhattan, New York, prime time live.

CHAPTER 27

▼

PART 1

Then moments later, as the crowd leans into this lifesaving attempt, a nearby crowd member, with an unpronounceable name, ever so quietly, cautiously, and slowly edges back, step by step, towards a safe position, yet maintains a clear view of the accident setting, the set.

***

And this person, with an unpronounceable name seems anatomically similar to a modern human, the overall appearance, and likely an aristocratic physicist, highly educated esthetic, philosophic soul, cultured, stately, dignified, discreet with a cool and calm demeanor of a supreme authority, based on the overall bearing and index of character.

***

Yet, this person seems different in other ways, such as, not related to the Mitochondrial Eve, mt-Eve, mt-MRCA, the matrilineal most recent common ancestor, or last tribe of, or tribes, of all currently living humans.

And in another way, this person seems different, as if someone who experienced decreased body mass, instability in the genome, swelling in major blood vessels, changes in eye shape, metabolism shifts, inflammation and alterations in his microbiome, and a strange lengthening of telomeres, the protective structures at the ends of chromosomes, as if an ultra-deep-space traveler, and those effects.

***

Then, a highly perceptive crowd member notices this unusual person, and again, then mumbles one impulse after another.

This person seems "a bit odd," such as "primitive," as if "from an unknown human species, quite so," and has an *otherness* quality; a concept in phenomenology.

So much so, this aristocratic seems as if a 10,000-, 25,000-year-old or more version of a human being, those primitive genetic traits, yet with a number of conditional gene knockouts.

***

As often in a big metropolitan city, people see an unusual person, very much so, yet without a question or serious investigation, a person lets the "issue" walk away, for various important reasons.

***

Nonetheless, here and now, this person with an unpronounceable name is a quick study, and represents an unknown humanlike species, the "reluctants," in every sense to the modern ways of civilization, to the modern version of progress, mostly a version forced by law, and laws made by a small fraction of people, and often by the powers-that-be to trap competition and the population; too often treat others as servants in a regimental system, who must obey or mimic on que; in yet another whim or popular experiment.

Such as, "Do, because I said so.

"Because, I make the laws," control the media, internet, impose pop culture, and/or one weird new social reality construct after another, and for a generation or more, that eventually develops into one ever so strange reality after another.

***

So historically, some human tribes, or humanlike, remain xenophobic, low key, disguised, others to the highest degree, and some ever so discreetly infiltrate the United States Government Policy and Supporting Positions, the Plum Book and K Street, United States capital of Washington, D.C, the Americas, Europe, Asia, Oceania, Polynesians and other region equivalents.

***

As often humans, especially the powerful, and on an impulse feel, then act to others, as if quite superior, and seek absolute control, such as expressed by *Manius Acilius,* a Roman general and consul of the Roman Republic in 191 BC, that the others were naturally meant to be enslaved with so many ways and means.

As if ever so sure, "certain people are born near worthless, because of gender, size, hair color, skin color, tribe, region, religion, economic system, nation-state system, or some other heuristic technique, a justification, an intuitive judgment, guesstimate, gut feeling, stereotype, common sense, profile; or of life as a mimic, or pack mule."

For, a simple grubstake?

For, one version of slavery or another, and that includes a wage slave, with one tenacious contractual obligation after another, and often for below-average water, food, safety, shelter, and more?

***

As compared to, a golden age of peace and prosperity, that ultimate golden age of heaven on earth, the next great k-wave, then ultimate universal harmonic wave; the longest period of stability in human history, a new version of classic Renaissance, Renaissance Humanism, Neoclassicism and the Age of Enlightenment, and the Romantic era version, the original long-lost glory now found.

And, a person can sit in a new version, classical, or Renaissance garden, a super bloom.

Sit within the nexus of philosophical secular and sacred space, then absorb apotropaic, transformative, and regenerative powers a pristine place; a place vivid, vital, free and fair; a place wholly natural and absolutely fascinating.

A special place for artists, poets, and scholars to sit then daydream venture.

▼

PART 2

And, while slowly backing to a safe position, that xenophobic quietly mumbles a strange language, of which seems to translate into, "So-called civilization, has had more than enough time to evolve from the muck, the petty; from cruel and usual, since the Stone Age, the Middle Paleolithic, such as 200,000 years ago, and that amount of time, with one social invention after another, of constructs, or the behaviorally modern human since 40–50,000 years ago, or a bible thumper may say, 10,000 years or so.

***

"Well, because it seems, as if these humans have been given enough time; more than enough time for real progress, a golden age.

***

"And, why make so many excuses for them, why grade them on curve again, and again, a bell-shaped curve, an education term for oh my, such slow learners, in fact dense. Or say another way, an impulsive, obtuse, stubborn, obsessive, and foolish mind.

"And what exactly have humans been doing for 200,000 years or so?"

***

So, this exceptional xenophobic representative, a quick study, an extraordinarily fast learner, especially of technology and game theory, gamification, ever so quietly, cautiously, slowly continues to edge back, to a safe position, yet maintains a clear view of the accident setting, the set in New York city, Manhattan, prime time live!

CHAPTER 28

▼

And this xenophobe, with an unpronounceable name seems fully prepared, knows a properly timed situation, then reaches inside a homemade bag, one that resembles a custom-made Tom Ford, T Line Grained Leather Weekender bag, as one exceptional crowd person and situation after another gather, then fully align to that accident, especially with cell phones, tablets, and wireless-enabled wearable technological devices and implants, also known as smart electronic devices that track GPS that related to vital real-time activity.

***

So much so, as this tremendous rush-hour crowd continues to build, it includes important players from various government, private and public organizations, such as Defense Advanced Research Projects Agency (DARPA), ETH Zürich, Pierre and Marie Curie University, University of Copenhagen, *Karolinska Institutet*, key member of the Federal United States House Committee on Oversight and Reform, University of Tokyo, United States Global Leadership Coalition member, a shadow cabinet member, corporate interlock, digerati, elite member of the Russell Aldwych Group, then certain vital aristocrats, and chivalrics.

The crowd also includes the famous dog whisperer, fantasy broker, professional chocolate taster, professional queuer for iPhones with colorful t-shirt that proudly advertises such, profession notetaker for very wealthy college legacy students, nude bingo announcer, and a fortune cookie writer who really hates cookies and is dressed as a philosopher of science Gottfried Wilhelm (von) Leibniz.

***

And, the dense crowd includes two other interesting people, especially a very famous wet nurse for the super wealthy and a well-respected balladeer, a troubadour similar to a *cicisbeatura* or *cicisbeismo* that has a well-established lineage over 800 years, to nobility in Genoa, Nice, Venice, Florence, and Rome.

***

And elsewhere, in the crowd, it includes five interesting people, a famous drug dealer disguised as the senior most Food and Drug Administration Office of Human Resources, maid, scruffy professional street beggar who is in fact quite wealthy, crocodile wrangler, and illegal immigrant with colorful t-shirt that proudly says so on both sides?

***

Also, in the crowd are four other unusual people, a professional crooner, ostrich babysitter dressed as a famous politician, dog food tester, and twitchy karate instructor.

***

And, on the other side of this dense crowd are six interesting people, which include a nude beach lifeguard, rabbi, maquillaphobic gem dealer, a well-known and followed clinically insane psychiatrist, opera singer dressed as Giuseppe Fortunino Francesco Verdi, and the highest paid professional mourner.

***

And, near them are a six other people, which include a construction worker, professional stand-in bridesmaid, well-known hairdresser for the elite with a dreadful *toupee*, professional smuggler, and a few everyday folks, such as wage slaves, working poor and debt bondage, the new-age version, where a job does not give a living wage or keep up with inflation year after year, or some other very complex situation, a *de facto* trap without the natural venting process of a true democracy and universal suffrage, a modern version of the poorhouse for a vast number of people.

***

And also, the crowd includes other shakers and movers, such as a prominent hedge fund manager, venture capitalist, banker, congressional committee member, acutely self-confident Sloane Ranger, political power broker, foil for the shadows, plenipotentiary, and a Davos person.

In addition, the crowd also includes other important people, such as from the *Global Plum Book*, transformative agent, unofficial senator, think tank member, 527 organization, political action committee, advocacy group, and Washington DC, K Street.

In addition, this crowd includes an honorary this or that, such as an ambassador, citizen, socialite and tastemaker, for example a studio system, a celebrity worship syndrome. Or say another way, a personality cult with groupies, and with a considerable fan base or fan site earns the equivalent of a Hugo Award for Best Fanzine.

Of equal note, the dense crowd includes a *Chambre Syndicale de la Haute Couture* member, fashionistas, fashion designer, makeup artist and a few exceptionally attractive fashion models who smell like heaven, and have magnificent curves, and who, one by one, squeeze their way thru the crowd towards that accident, and squeeze between.

***

So much so, and eventually, they squeeze by an ever so serious professional grump, also known as a glum, grump, frump and mugwump, a person known for poverty, a bounded function, a poverty of one idea after another, the histaminic, or a tightly wound histone, a repression, a churn, a person who believes in the good old days, and "Old times were good times." A person who specializes taking full advantage of the poor, middle, or if need be, upper class, as a sport, profession, and industry.

Of which, might eventually displace a generation or two, for instance "Investment Riches Built on Subprime Auto Loans to Poor."

Or, other classic ways and means to earn, such as the good old days, by exploiting the weak, an impulse to do so. Then act to others as if quite superior, and seek absolute control. Such as expressed by Manius Acilius, a Roman general and consul of the Roman Republic in 191 BC, and others, that the "others" were naturally meant to be enslaved with so many ways and means? As if ever so sure, certain people are born near worthless, because of gender, size, hair color, skin color, tribe, region, religion, economic system, nation-state system, or some other heuristic technique, a justification, an intuitive judgment, guesstimate, gut feeling, stereotype, common sense, profile. So, life as a mimic of this philosophy, or cheerleader, such as "kiss up, and kick down," kick a pack mule, or someone looking for a simple grubstake. And, "Old times were good times."

Or put another way, to earn a living, believe in an enemy-of-the month club.

Or put another way, by stepping on the ant, and that chain of events, and mash, really mash, and grind, and grind.

Or, hit the monkey and win a cookie.

CHAPTER 29

▼

INTERMISSION: SON OF DAVE, "OLD TIMES WERE GOOD TIMES"?

And, that grumpy philosophy may remind a person, who truly believes the official song video, Son of Dave, "Old times Were Good Times"?

▼

PART 1

Yet, as one exceptionally attractive fashion model after another, and another, slowly squeezes by the grump, this man sees and smells heaven on earth.

***

So much so, the grump now believes in paradise, then fascinates, ogles each and every contour of one model after another, immediately feels tremendous relief from years of an ever so certain grumpy mindset, that cumulative effect of so much gristle, of ugh, disgust of most situations, of ideas, people, places, and things, other than that mindset.

As if too much of a certain protein or more, a DNA manufacturing problem, too much production of a certain protein, or more.

That creates a cumulative feeling of, grump, ugh, disgust.

Then impulse to clip something, pause, or block something internally.

Yet often, grump does so externally, to an idea, people, place, things, or clip out an entire species, so what people die?

***

As a result, here and now, above all other internal feelings, moods, from the sight of these models, this grump feels happy, playful, and a bit silly as eyebrows wiggle.

***

Of which, it seems out of character for this person, as a mood lasting years has a cumulative effect on the mind, body, soul, and something not easily changed.

Yet now, it greatly transforms this person.

CHAPTER 30

▼

PART 2

And slowly, as the last model tries to squeeze by the grump, his thoughts speed, offers her a golden smile, closes eyes, then kiss.

▼

PART 3

However, the last exceptionally attractive fashion model notices, seriously distresses, seems quite worried, as the closed-eyed professional grump's puckered lips approach.

▼

PART 4

So, in this ever so tight crowd and quickly, this gorgeous model looks about for ideas here and there.

***

Then quite desperate, she quietly picks up a nearby puppy and uses it as a kiss substitute, and again, then departs.

CHAPTER 30

▼

PART 5

Of which, this apparently fools the professional grump, whose eyes eventually open, face delights to no end, and truly gushes, then launches into a very long and ever so charming speech, a soliloquy, to no one in particular, and says, "Ah, yes.

"Now, this is the new golden age of peace, paradise, that ultimate golden age of heaven on earth, peace and prosperity, the next great k-wave then ultimate universal harmonic wave, the longest period of stability in human history, a new version of classic Renaissance, Renaissance Humanism, Neoclassicism and the Age of Enlightenment, and the Romantic era version, yes, the original long-lost glory now found; maybe *Stabiae*? or some other cultural equivalent.

"And, I can sit in a new version of a classical and Renaissance garden.

"Sit within the nexus of philosophical secular and sacred space, then absorb apotropaic, transformative, and regenerative powers a pristine place, a place vivid, vital, free and fair, a place wholly natural and absolutely fascinating.

"A special place for artists, poets, and scholars to sit then daydream venture, yes, and let the mind wander to solve some great mystery, or mentally drift, such as drift on an ever so slow peaceful wave.

"All of which, gives this place a certain image of prosperity, progress and peace, a place in full accord with nature, as if it represents an unofficial paradise, a steady state, such as two, three: four!"

CHAPTER 31

▼

PART 1

Moments later, in the dense crowd, on the nearby ground, and facing the grump, that puppy barks, then offers an exceptionally playful happiness, "Arf, arf, arf!"
So much so, the tail wags, then really wags.

***

And it causes the previous grump, to immediately snap out that daydream speech, carefully look about, then at the puppy, seriously frown, sizzle, and boldly say and point elsewhere, "Stay away!

***

"Stay over there.
"I don't like dogs, especially puppies, as they quickly find trouble.
"Or, they create it, as in dogmatic."

***

As a result, the puppy sees and hears, as if a full measurement, and immediately feels wounded, then true hopelessness, as if forsaken and abandoned from society.

***

And eventually, one magnificent fashion model after another, who smells as if heaven on earth, squeezes by another person, then another, and arrives up front, to closely view the accident.

***

And all the while, in this dense crowd, a few famous fashionistas and hauterflies huddle, scan, and study one crowd member after another head to toe.

▼

PART 2

Then, with ultimate insider fashionista language comments, well known to their "sect," in every sense of that word, they take turns, and utter a first impression blurt; also known as an impulse.

And that leads to, mostly one well-crafted verbal nip, peck, and blunt critique after another—as if everyone, and everything appears "fair game" to this criticism technique, and especially formulated; to raise or wither one target after another, as if in or out of existence.

＊

And moments later, nearby, some of their best fashionista friends notice them, seriously wave, offer a genuinely warm smile, as if long-lost glory now found, then move towards, squeeze by one person after another, with a louder than reasonable slightly annoyed voice, "Excuse me."

"No, excuse us."

"No.

"Pardon me."

"Yes."

"Yes, pardon me.

"We have emergency."

And, that allows one ever so narrow squeeze thru after another.

"Thank you.

"Yes, thank you."

Then, "Oops, I didn't mean to touch you there—honestly.
"You seem nice, very.
"And I like you, yet not that much."

***

So much so, these fashionistas and hauterflies meet, offer an exceptional heartfelt welcome, warm hugs, unconditional joy, and ever so intimate eye contact, then over-the-top praise to each other.

CHAPTER 31

▼

PART 3

However, in that new fashion group, a woman says quite excited, "We must go.

"This is yet another urgent moment, as the four fashion world capitals of Milan, Paris, New York and London, as well as Portugal, Rome, São Paulo, and Berlin converge here, at New York Fashion Week.

"And, did you hear what Michael Kors said yesterday?

"And, I fully expect Bottega Veneta to offer an oh my goodness, and Alexander Wang to deliver yet another spectacular range of wow.

"Plus, the food should be magnificent, and as Kaia Gerber brings yet another breakout runway star, a person to watch, a tastemaker extraordinaire."

***

And that new group fashionista member becomes overly excited, continues, then says as eyes widen, as if into the promise land, "Ji Won Choi, Daniel Cloke, Jamall Osterholm, Mara Hoffman, and Pamella Roland.

***

"And, this week includes Tadashi Shoji, John Elliott, Christopher John Rogers, Ulla Johnson, Jonathan Cohen …

"… Kim Shui, Nicole Miller, Jeremy Scott, and Kith."

▼

Part 4

Then from sheer excitement, the fashionista member hyperventilates.

So much so, another new group member says, "Slow down, sister.

"Slow down.

"Breathe."

Yet she continues, "And today features Tory Burch, Kate Spade, Hellessy, Snow Xue Gao, and Jason Wu, then Linder, Milly, Paul Andrew, Cushnie, and Monse.

***

"Then later, we can see Chromat, Vivienne Hu, The Blonds, Marina Moscone, Taoray Wang, and Dion Lee.

"Then if very lucky, we can see R13, Yuna Yang, Son Jung Wan, Eckhaus Latta, Christian Cowan, Longchamp, then Christian Siriano, Brandon Maxwell, Détacher, Pyer Moss, and...."

CHAPTER 31

▼

PART 5

Then from hyperventilation and sheer excitement, that group fashionista member shows a wild-eyed groupie craze, a real out-of-mind look, followed by complete calm, then concern, worry, alarm, panic, evasive, petrified, then calm, acceptance, satisfied, happy, elated, and a profound realization arrives, then giddy, as she now appears clinically insane.

***

So much so, in a wholly unnatural way, eyes roll about, she passes out, falls backwards, then impacts with an ungainly thud, as feet fly high into the air.

***

And, something no person should experience, especially when wearing a dress, an impeccable one from Brunello Cucinelli, Akris, or is it from Chloe of New York City?

CHAPTER 32

▼

As a result, the fashionistas see, jaws drop, eyes widen, as their fate, destiny, karma, luck, randomness of nature, the Pauli effect, that philosophy, or another, that way of life and conditioning, such as social conditioning; as a neo-romance aesthetic; of which includes the Platonic notions of beauty, spirit, freedom, and justice; the potential of individual creativity, aspirations, and opportunity, and full restoration of the lost glory: and very particular expressions and compelling degrees of transcendence.

***

And, this fallen fashionista seems as if, a wild-eyed crazed groupie, clinically insane.

***

Yet, these other fashionistas watch, as if frozen in thought.

***

As before, they remember this phenomenon.

It often happens to overworked fashionistas, hauterflies, designers, and other people who truly obsess about the standard of true greatness; and obsess, and obsess, then some become clinically insane, some become a withered bit, a smaller self, yet more mental knots, a trouble tree.

***

So much so, here and now, they cringe at the thought, and again, then one of them mumbles, "This could happen to me.

"Oh my.

"Yes."

***

Yet, they do nothing significant, to help that passed-out friend, who fell backwards, then impacted with an ungainly thud, as feet flew high into the air, and something no person should experience, especially when wearing a dress, an impeccable one from Brunello Cucinelli, Akris, or is it from Chloe?

***

They do not, quickly elbow someone out of the way, so as, to get into a lifesaving position, check for signs of life, the pulse, blood pressure, respiratory rate, body temperature, and for any other sign of life.

***

Then moments later, group members hear a distant voice, and another, and another, that maybe Michael Kors, Diane von Furstenberg, Carolina Herrera, Oscar de la Renta, Calvin Klein, Ralph Lauren, and Isaac Mizrahi?

***

As a result, that passed-out fashionista's eyes open quite wide, then she says, "Isaac Mizrahi?"

CHAPTER 33

▼

And suddenly fully energized, super alert and motivated, the downed fashionista quickly pops up, to a standing position, triangulates again, and again, of where Isaac Mizrahi's voice came from, yet cannot see, because of the dense Manhattan accident crowd.

Nor can she see, what perhaps, is Michael Kors, Diane von Furstenberg, Carolina Herrera, Oscar de la Renta, Calvin Klein, or Ralph Lauren.

***

As a result, she and the other new group members, seem ever so abrupt, bid goodbye to those other fashionistas and hauterflies.

***

Then with urgency, they depart and squeeze thru the crowd, and often, along the way, say with a voice much louder than reasonable, and considerably annoyed, "Excuse me.

"Pardon me.

"Yes, pardon me,

"Thank you.

"Yes, thank you.

"Oops, I didn't mean to touch you there—honestly.

"You seem nice, very.

"And I like you, yet not that much.

"Or do I", as eyes narrow, as if maybe a found paradise.

Yet their mission is to find, then serve the finest fashion authority, someone gifted, a leading spokesperson, author, or auctor of the industry, a spiritual and moral insight, for one utterly divine inspired revelation after another, from spiritual truth prophetic, who foretells the future, as a prophet, or is it profit, *profectus, proficere*; or better yet, the origin of, an original, *oriri*, an *ab initio*; and to rise; yes, one small victory after another!

CHAPTER 34

▼

PART 1

And, with these thoughts, new group fashionistas and hauterflies members squeeze by one crowd member after another, in search of an original, yes, exceptional, and not a mistranslation, not a cheap imitation.

As they search for what seems as if Michael Kors, Diane von Furstenberg, Carolina Herrera, Oscar de la Renta, Calvin Klein, Ralph Lauren, and Isaac Mizrahi.

***

Then with urgency, they continue to squeeze thru the crowd, and often, along the way, say with a voice much louder than reasonable and considerably annoyed "Excuse me."

"No, excuse us.

"Yes.

"Pardon me.

"Yes, pardon us.

"We have emergency."

And, one at a time, that allows each of them an ever so narrow squeeze-thru.

"Thank you."

"Yes, thank you."

Then, "Oops, I didn't mean to touch you there—honestly.

"You seem nice, very.

"And I like you, yet not that much."

CHAPTER 34

▼

Part 2

Then moments later, the original fashionistas and hauterflies group, that offered heartfelt emotions, warm hugs, unconditional joy, and ever so intimate eye contact to friends, they in great detail, and one at a time harshly criticize the fashion sense, mannerisms, and other traits of those newly departed best friends.

***

So much so, to nearby crowd outside observers, it seems a quite hypocritical and exceedingly cruel.

CHAPTER 34

▼

PART 3

And eventually, because the accident delays this commute, they grow quite frustrated, then focus on one nearby crowd member after another, especially their fashion sense, mannerism and other traits, then offer group members a whisper, clever ultimate insider verbal zinger, mocking phrase, and partially restrained blurt laugh, that causes other people to notice.

***

Then the fashionistas and hauterflies grow bold, especially because of their numbers, that maybe a universal phenomenon, the addictive power of a herd, a swarm at the tipping point, or virtuous circle and vicious circle.

And soon, they seem unable or unwilling to manage their voice volume, which gradually changes from *pianississimo*, or extremely soft, to *fortissimo*, very loud, that only adds to the tipping point at this dense accident scene, the set.

Especially, as they say raw comments about whoever comes into focus,
"British teeth."

"1661."

"Trout pout."

"AMW."

"Foot facelift."

"Chicken cutlet."

***

So much so, and each time, in delivering pain, most of these group members seem a bit smug, and find great pleasure announcing a found flaw or more.

***

And they announce as if, they have finally reached their full potential as a human, to quickly label, as if a blunt truth-telling sage, or wilderness guide.

▼

PART 4

And, in their professional opinion, if the label inflicts punishment that sticks for a lifetime, so be it; as truth seems more important.

***

As a result, most of these comments seem as if, designed to embarrass, shame, and damage a reputation, or insert rot; such as to mark that person as an outsider, the other, or worse yet, as an it or thing.

***

All of which, gives the impression of well-educated thugs or bullies, yet not a common thug, who stands on the other spectrum end, and with a kinetic solution, with brute force of a fistic.

As various forms of thugs and bullies specialize in tormenting the opposition, especially the weak, as both use impulse, inflation, overbear, bluster, and grow bold in numbers.

***

Yet for some of these fashionistas and hauterflies, it resembles an overly sensitive thin skin of a self-absorbed prickly me, a being easily to irritate;

easy to tip that personality system, such as with a very small piece of lint, cat hair, lack of fashion, or something else.

And a person, who uses one sly impulse technique after another, to intimidate others with a peck, or as an obsessive; such as the art of deliberately planting something; planting rot, or make something barren, that maybe, the thing these speakers fear the most; that attack technique by others?

***

So, they nip first?

Or say another way, attack first, a first strike, with that cycle of escalation, misunderstanding, and turmoil, then puzzle about the petty others?

***

And, do most fashionistas and hauterflies have "thin skin," overly sensitive feelings?

Or say another way, aesthetic feelings, as if a DNA manufacturing problem or benefit, too much production of a certain protein, or more?

***

And in general, why does a person/system, especially fashionistas and hauterflies expect everyone to live as if a complete, timeless, exceptional fashion-forward system; the ideal version of right and wrong, such as perfection 24/7/365...

..., or is it 365.2425, or 365.25, 365.25636, 365.242189; and as if an ever ready; of which seems obsessive?

***

And why do fashionistas and hauterflies expect everyone to dress as if a spellbinding event, with all those situational adjustments, on the fly, such as based on an idea, mood, theme, and/or event daily, week, month, and season?

And these fashionistas and hauterflies seem to aspire and live as if a guardian of aesthetic, and if need be, a harsh or captious judge of value, truth, righteousness, beauty, and technique; as a professional or a wantabe.

That delivers an acute analysis, evaluation, and appreciation of art or an artistic performance; often deliberating as if a drama critic, a reliable, gifted *savant*, maybe Orpheus, Ὀρφεύς, a Thracian, or some other cultural equivalent; such as a truth-telling fresh-start specialist.

And if need be, charm all living things.

And maybe charm a stone, or piles of into an exceptional life, such as, if need be, revive a stone or calcified thing, maybe an idea, character, philosophy, function, setting, or system.

Or at the minimum, make it into something that is in full accord with a system, or better yet, the universe, that skill set.

***

CHAPTER 35

▼

Suddenly, David shows some signs of life, moves ever so slightly, and again, breathes, and again, moans a bit, then conks out, yet better described as he croaks, as if truly dead.

▼

Part 1

All the while, that xenophobe with an unpronounceable name cautiously, slowly, and quietly edges back, towards a safe position, seems fully prepared, and knows a properly timed situation.

As here and now at this accident, one exceptional person and situation after another gathers then fully aligns to that accident, especially with cell phones, tablets, and wireless-enabled wearable technological devices and electronic implants, also known as smart electronic devices that track GPS that related to vital real-time activity.

***

So much so, this tremendous rush-hour crowd includes very important players from various government, private and public institutions, in addition to quite unique and common individuals.

As this situation seems an ideal representative grouping, a grouplike structure, groupoid, or abelian group within a daily Manhattan "commute," and commute in every sense of the word.

And, as nearly all of these accident crowd members have no idea about the new age farm system, of data farming techniques, the next great zeitgeist, the related major mystery breakthru, such as related to unsolved problems of personal contacts, chats, confidential files, corporate secrets, habits, obsessions, how to compel someone to buy yet continually ignore self-interest, and regarding the other vital problems in physics, chemistry, biology, medicine, and music theory, of rhythm, melody, structure, form, texture, especially universal harmonics, supramolecular chemistry, molecular self-assembly, molecular folding, and molecular recognition.

***

In addition, in this accident crowd, many of these people seemed trapped in a new version of the rat race.

Or say another way, trapped in a new age farm crop cycle, as measured by an ever so complex web farm, a complex entanglement, of the ever so long game associated with the human species and the universe.

***

And to that xenophobe, civilization and especially powers-that-be seem obsessive, the obsessiveness many systems expect 24/7, as if an addiction mentality, of groupthink, especially group pander.

And, they expect group members to pander on cue, as if a professional pander, and basest emotions; expect a quick-change artist, yet to a fault; and often into a trope, a stereotype, or typical bias; such as the forty to fifty common cognitive biases, as one loyalty test after another; yet not loyal to the members, as members seem quite disposable.

***

And, to that xenophobe, all of which relates to an infinitely long game, determinacy, differential games, such as the continuous pursuit and evasion of an asymmetric and metagame, often in search of a red herring or unobtainium, and that endless expensive chase, into a tighter and tighter quandary.

CHAPTER 36

▼

PART 2

And to the xenophobe, for the smallest things, civilization seems quite petty, promotes trivial, and serves so many masters said sacred, with so many mixed messages, as if in a robust netcentric yet very cold war, and what one expects in truly unconventional and asymmetric warfare, especially the psychological warfare of economics.

Of which uses the frequent use of thrownness, phase transition, poor seam management, emergence, swarm behavior, spontaneous symmetry breaks, convection cells, and real-time stochastic calculus.

And often, as if deliberately so, civilization lacks reasonable and promote a panderer in accord with a powerful interest.

***

And, it seems deliberate, to dumb down and make petty, the roll of media, such as live in the stage between preadolescence and adolescence, that volatile region of one major change, challenge, and anxiety after another, then repeat that pattern, often made so by law then groupthink.

***

At least it seems so according to this xenophobe, with an unpronounceable name, who appears as if an extraordinarily fast learner, especially of technology, game theory, gamification.

***

Or, if you prefer greater detail, this xenophobe specializes in the abelian groupoid, associativity, identity, invertibility, commutativity, and those other major categories mostly hidden, yet as if more than a four-dimensional thinking, such as a manifold tendency, that systematic effort, "to fold onto itself, pressurize, and entangle;" and infinite dimensional manifold systems of, orbifold(s), and spherical harmonics of degree n = 5 or so tendency.

And, how they related to forecasting, especially top-priority financial stock and option trades, such as the next super stocks, total conviction buy signs, gap-up-stocks, breakout potentials, greatly undervalued, and wide moat stocks.

CHAPTER 37

▼

Meanwhile, with two united fists, the doctor pounds on *Erika*'s chest, and again.

***

And moments later, she gasps, and again, then takes one deep breath after another, and another, then a final last breath.

So much so, one crowd member after another serves as a witness.

CHAPTER 38

▼

As a result, this xenophobe cautiously moves further away.

Again, this person seems a bit odd, such primitive, as if from an unknown humanlike species, quite unusual, and has an "otherness" quality, a concept in phenomenology.

CHAPTER 39

▼

Yet in this case, that xenophobe seems quite similar to a modern human appearance, and somehow an aristocrat.

As often in a big metropolitan city, people see an unusual person, very much so.

However, let the "issue" walk away without a serious investigation, for various reasons.

***

And, this xenophobe continues to step back, and cautiously pokes inside a homemade bag, one that resembles a custom-made Tom Ford, T Line Grained Leather Weekender bag, then retrieves something larger and much thicker than a cell phone, more robust, shock-resistant, rugged, and can submerge underwater over forty fathoms.

Yet much of that extra thickness has some additional unknown functions.

And, the phone like device has a six-inch full HD screen, that appears as if 1920x1080 pixels at 401 ppi or so.

And, the device has various ever so complex heavily segmented attachments on what seems as if a bank of micro-USB 5.0 sub ports.

So much so, these attachments seem quite difficult to describe, such as beyond all description categories, and as if each segment has a vital scientific function, yet from this angle not viewable.

***

Then moments later, that xenophobe's eyes narrow, and all the while, discreetly look about for danger, especially one vital crowd member after another.

Then, something clicks, slides, and other sounds occur, yet sounds most modern people would not notice, as people far removed from the subtle aspects of nature. As these sounds warn of a disaster.

And, wild animals would notice, then flee without protest, as they know something is coming, something very bad, and based on that special wild animal sense.

Then something else happens.

Something.

CHAPTER 40

▼

As a result, and carefully without notice, the xenophobe backs into something attached to a building, a six-foot-wide, nine-foot-tall, and three-foot-deep thing, a lightweight portable building addition, one easy for a person to maneuver into this place, and a maneuverable quite difficult to describe.

***

Also, this attached thing, the portable building addition, has some traits of a Colonial *Baroque* niche, in the *La Merc*ed district, Mexico City, yet with much more elaborate details.

And, this thing has an entrance three feet wide and six feet high.

Yet, it seems impossible to see inside, at one angle after another, then one ever so close look after another, especially the seams.

And, how is that possible, an entrance with no clear or systematic ability to enter?

***

And outside, it resembles more of a portable secular aedicula, with a central niche, a "shrine" entrance, as defined before the twelfth century with the word *scrin*, from Latin *scrinium*, a case, chest, or receptacle; a place or object hallow by association, especially a sacred relic deposit or sanctuary, a place devoted to a secular or religious idea, object, person, patron, saint, deity, situation, system, and/or theme.

Or say another way, a place that offers perspective, setting, system, emergent phenomena, the harmonics, and solves the classic "symmetric hierarchy problem," a "moduli space classification."

Or say another way, a place that offers a metathetic storyline.

Or say another way, a place that offers Roman à clef?

Or say another way, a place that offers a theatre, meromorphic function, bureaucracy, offset, distance, displacement, volume, shape, pattern, potential, and set then return home: as a special case.

Or say another way, a place that offers a complex focal point, a tethering system, of which often pulls a person far away from their original intent and natural aspiration, with one more restricted degrees of freedom after another?

CHAPTER 41

▼

Then moments later, as a southeast wind whips thru, menacing clouds billow to great heights, as if to an immense anvil shape, this xenophobe carefully looks about the dense crowd, especially at an elite member of Defense Advanced Research Projects Agency (DARPA), ETH Zürich, Pierre and Marie Curie University, University of Copenhagen, and Karolinska Institutet.

And sees a key member of the Federal United States House Committee on Oversight and Reform, University of Tokyo, United States Global Leadership Coalition member, a shadow cabinet member, corporate interlock, digerati, elite member of the Russell Aldwych Group, then certain vital aristocrats and chivalrics.

Until a twitchy, unemployed black belt karate instructor accidentally blocks the line of sight.

***

All the while, that Norwegian Nobel Committee member, new Swedish Academy committee secretary, and permanent seasoned adviser well known in Scandinavia as "the specialist" continue towards the accident, and squeeze pass one person after another, then pass that famous dog whisperer who is often ignored, especially regarding basic communications, habits and responsibilities.

CHAPTER 42

▼

PART 1

INSIDE THAT NICHE

Note: a typical reader should skip this chapter, unless a super geek or nerd *extraordinaire* interested in a real-time stream of observations, of raw thoughts, as the events happen so quickly, in fragments, of raw observations notes, with best effort descriptives.

Then, the xenophobe carefully looks about, verifies no witnesses, not even a pet, who could reveal this, or at least part of the secret process.

***

And, to the entrance, this person does something, yet not clearly visible, then enters, secures the door, and looks inside a huge room that defy physics, as compared to the outside.

And how is that possible?

***

The outside measurements are six-foot-wide, nine-foot-tall, and three-foot-deep, lightweight, portable building addition.

Yet inside seems forty times larger, or more, or even more, yet not well lit, especially right, left, and in back.

***

And, this person searches inside the niche for resources, at one densely complex archive pillar library after another, mathematical objects, the best of the best field-programmable gate arrays, programmable logic blocks, a hierarchy of reconfigurable interconnects, ...

... complex combinational functions, a superior class of automata, digital infinities, generative linguistics, origin of language, the universe, ...

... populated by strange things and resources quite difficult to describe, yet imply the "fundamentals" of classic and hidden reserves, such as a normal reader should skip this chapter, unless a super geek or nerd extraordinaire.

***

And these pillars on each side form a great arc, to the door well system, a field-programmable gate array, programmable logic blocks, a hierarchy of reconfigurable interconnects, complex combinational functions, that often contains molecular knots, the best of the best, a superior class of automata, epigenome regulators, digital infinity.

Then, a closer look at one wall after another reveals so many oddly complex imbedded things, world within worlds, especially close up here and there, and implies, at the smallest level, the work of a master quantum mechanics, resonance-phenomenon-natural frequency, collectively exhaustive events, oneiromancy outlier events, and open source higher-order functions.

***

As this niche does something quite unusual, such as "emanation" in many senses of the word, yet some definitions not listed in the dictionary.

And, it produces a series of unusual "hierarchically ascending radiations" from a substantial unknown source, not easy to locate, as if everywhere, yet not so, and from a massive hidden thing.

Or say another way, someone has tampered with the fundamental laws of nature.

And again, nearly all of which, in this niche, this aedicula, seems quite difficult to accurately describe.

For instance, when an idea, philosophy, mission statement, party platform, war, or system looks and sounds good in the beginning, because it seems attractive or vital, and has a certain gravitas, such as sugar, starch, or yeast?

However, the deployment represents a very tricky process, a true struggle—which takes on a life of its own, develops mission creep then complex legacy, and requires a complicated process to keep it from bloat, from obsession then distraction, from lack of focus.

***

And inside this niche, it seems as if a world within a world and great detail, a farm system, with many complex devices, and some seem almost human—confused, disoriented, isolated then forsaken, and in a profound identity crisis, identity foreclosure, a critical phase transition during the great identity versus role crisis of the self...

... such as multiple identities in one person, roles, loyalties, invertibilities, commutativity, and those other major identity categories mostly hidden within a mind.

***

Such as, here and now, in this niche, will these human like people survive from all this experimentation, from this new golden age of biological, chemical, material and subspace manipulation, especially from plastics, the consumption of?

And how does a system digest plastic, and think about it, as plastic seems to circulate everywhere, particularly within the mind, body, and soul?

***

So much so, here and now, inside this niche, the entire system undergoes a profound mortal suffering.

***

And yet, the process has a certain brilliant glory that seems universal, classic and profound, which radiates from it, in a series of very particular expressions and compelling degrees, as if the entire system sits at some fundamental threshold, at the very edge of existence.

***

Or, put another way, when a person or thing has a tremendous sense of alienation, as someone who barely survived a war, still feels numb, and things around take on a pale, empty, and surreal look, then personal demons, painful memories and regrets rush forward along with a full realization.

They have become the other, become an it, and have entered the great unknown, that great frontier, and will face a true mystery, …

… that often needs a familiar song, a classic aria, strophic, madrigal, or cue, or something that may resemble "Max Manus OST – 18" by Trond Bjerknes, that helps document a tremendous sense of isolation, and loneliness.

CHAPTER 42

▼

PART 2

Then, something else happens, something.

***

And moments later, inside this niche, the xenophobe begins a complex ritual, then directs it mid room, at various tall, substantial, odd "stacks," for lack of a better description.

***

So much so, this ritual seems quite serious, and difficult to describe one stage after another, such as it may be a self-imposed ritual, special situation appropriate evocation, or rite of passage.

***

And this xenophobe says as if casting an evocation rhythm, a spell, "a major transformation, from aspects here and there that seem as if an undifferentiated totality, from primordial substance, and into energy, life, spirit and glory: a mystery of resurrection, and new beginning, a temporal adjustment, a certain truth, and rise from this place, oh noble spirit, rise, rise!"

CHAPTER 42

▼

PART 3

PUBLISHER NOTE: A CHAPTER COMPONENT,
DELIBERATELY WITHHELD BY THE WRITER

▼

PART 4

Then moments later, inside this niche, a closer look at one stack after another gives the impression of tall, odd stone, with heavily populated outcrops, of various minerals or mineraloids, as if a lithospheric upper growth phenomenon, a special crop.

Yet these stacks also contain biological, technological, and other materials, that in total resemble a major transformation, as if a comprehensive spectacular metaplasia transcending.

***

And all the while, on them, various creatures great and small live, and meticulously maintain these things, of worlds within worlds that thrive.

***

And, in the niche, off to the side, sits an odd "thing," for lack of a better description, that includes a rhombicosidodecahedral workstation.

Of which, much of it seems alive, and a place to sit inside, yet as if part of that thing, a function of, another component, and face ever so complex creatures, devices, computer screens, panels, and keyboards like no known system.

▼

PART 5

And, several computer screens monitor real-time data updates, that show an ever so complex metagame, a grand strategic "physical system" and differential game of continuous pursuit and evasion, as the play of one game develops the rules for another game.

Such as, it shows one area of mathematics after another, of infinitary combinatorics, probabilistic forecasting, ensemble forecasting, especially game theory, yet, as if the ultimate metagame, an experimental Delphic-Bayesian game theory expanse.

It shows gamification, game-design elements, principles, techniques, and one storyline arc after another, of possibilities, an endless ability, such as avoid this system, go for literal and figurative low hanging fruit.

As this system maybe the original of everything, the universe.

So, trifle with someone else, the disadvantage, a race, creed, religion, idea, or other construct.

As many of this niche system applied to one vital nongame situation after another, to the stock market, crowdsourcing, traffic, voter redistricting, and superior gerrymandering, not to some normal or crude effort.

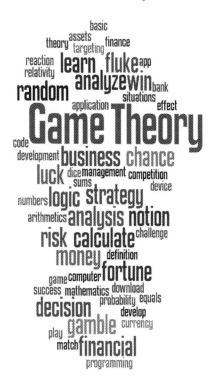

And, other computer screens seem to track vital players on the invisible internet and World Wide Web, especially the vast dark web, the main system tree trunk, essential roots, and branches that extend with activity not visible with traditional web search engines, such as Google, Baidu, Yahoo, Bing, Excite, or Ask ...

... especially not shown by internet providers, businesses, and governments; with their special commercial, economic, and political interests, such as what they want you to see, see their worldview, and believe, really believe, mimic, speak, as easily as a lyrebird sings, or oriole, mimic thrushes, tanagers ...

✳✳✳

... such as shape your reality, as if the only reality, and often expect you to say so on cue, and systematically block other views, other worldviews, perspectives, other nonstandard models of the community, region, state, nation, world, and universe ...

... and block other reference tools, versions of reality, especially physics, such as other nonstandard models of physics ...

... other ways and means to see reality.

Yet often, what they offer seems overly complex, full of contradictions, and ever so shallow, as if a flat thing, in so many ways.

***

Just as importantly, these niche workstation computer "terminals," and terminals in every known sense of the word, including origin of, track vital players, track those who can trigger a major rollback event, then removal of insider privilege ...

... that competitive chase, the "competitive exclusion principle" in action, and all those laws and rules, many designed to block a competitor, with so many barriers, one after another, with complex entanglements.

***

And the vast majority of people, systems, and things might never know; all those rules, laws, and exceptions ...

... with so many wait-on-a-branch techniques, trapped in a competitive chase, or wait in the poorhouse, to find the next vital and sustainable branch.

***

And, of equal or greater importance, another workstation computer screen monitors, and another show other world systems, that seem quite complex, the typical, normal, that have a certain staleness, and flatness, of each worldview.

Or, said another way, each seems as if a faithfully flat scheme, cohomology, that treats people and other systems as if generic property, a conditional gene knockout or more, in a process that demands a "faithfully flat fundamental descent," of which, eventually fades, into a sober, yet ever so complex reality, of stuck again, in another quagmire?

***

And, other workstation computer screens track financial markets, especially liquidity in regular, grey, dark, and black pools ...

... of which, stream private security trades, not shown to the public, and not thru public stock exchanges, and one effort after another, to hide by the elite, the "a-list," by ultimate insiders, such as vital players, families, and institutions.

***

In addition, this niche system shows context, real-time, then ultimate insider ways and means, such as how they secretly communicate, code words, phrases, stock trade secrets, and seasonal timing.

▼

PART 6

Then, another workstation computer screen tracks creeds for sale.

***

And, one computer screen tracks one key individual and system after another, the internet providers, businesses and governments ...

... tracks those that create and maintain their own storyline, such as the reality, they try to sell with the latest campaign with techniques and tricks.

As if, each reality is a bubble ...

... bubble physics ...

... as life inside each has certain dynamics, and techniques to sustain.

***

And, another screen tracks how each relates to one another, those dynamics, especially:

1) The universe, the ultimate bubble expansion
2) The most important objects in the universe
3) Gauge theory reference level differentiations that measure the "rise over run" and customizing one problem after another, for a fair comparison

4) Regulated redundant degrees of freedom in the Lagrangian, as an extra circle, a fiber is added on every point of sphere, to create a three-sphere, such as to describe the motion of particles, of a solid or fluid in continuum mechanics

5) Tetrahedron invariant under twelve distinct rotations, with reflections included, and shown in a real-time cycle graph format, along with the 180° edge and 120° vertex rotations that permute the tetrahedron thru the positions

6) The knotted object internet providers, businesses, and governments promote, then roll into existence, such as these rotating matrices throw off circles, knotted objects, three space fibers over the two sphere...

... based on a 720-degree rotation throw method; and each effort is shown on the workstation computer monitors as stereographic projection.

... as humans are often gerrymandered, stripped of one freedom after another, until a person is yet another dull component, a throwaway component ...

... throw away, a family, gender, friend, tribe, team, employer, town, politic, culture, religion, race, or other social constructs, or worse yet, treats them as a thing or an "it," or as a cash cow, inside yet another rut.

Then the system truly shocks, or pretends to, especially the media, when a small percent of the oppressed radicalize from systematically poor treatment, enormous pressure, and become the enemy.

As if, the system and media have profound bias, a fair weather friend, I took you so, to melodrama, hype, a few silver coins, and with no longer term memory.

Of which, seems a lesson rarely learned thru the history of the human species.

Yet enterprise does great things. It does truly great things.

However, in that rush to gain tremendous treasure, a certain dilemma exists, when tinkering—and tinkering according to that classic definition, especially on vital systems, fundamental building blocks, and components, as the experimental gerrymandered process—produces a considerable amount of waste and "whatnot."

***

And this story is about a certain "whatnot," as well as the great biological mystery, and untranslatability functions of nature, beyond all language, often underappreciated by a person, system or set of, in search of the next K-wave.

***

And in this case, at least according to the computer screens, the worldwide internet providers, businesses, and governments attempt to create each and every reality, that results in a "dangerously engaging" game among these interests, and sucked into one mind game after another …

… especially the ultimate mind game, or game theory, gamification, bundle theory, of obsession, escalation, paranoia, and purity, a quandary, catch-22, Cornelian dilemma, or Pyrrhic victory-based system, as compared to the opposite philosophy, a golden age of peace, prosperity, and tranquility.

***

Of which, few internet providers, businesses and governments seriously promote the golden age of peace, of fairness, reasonable…

… to usher in the next truly great branch for the human species, a 250-year golden age of peace and prosperity …

… the greatest expansion of peace and prosperity in the history for the human species?

CHAPTER 42

▼

PART 7

Then another computer screen, if you could call it that, as it has several organic components, and gives the full impression of a directorate.

Of which, it shows one projected sphere of influence and control after another, inside the niche, and a system, that deploys bait in various complex pits, snares, torment of shadows, substance, and other wiles, especially for anyone that illegally enters the niche system.

***

In addition, the computer screens show a far-reaching ability, to carefully deliver measured influence overseas, with an exceptional ability, to smoothly enter the ways and means of institutional machinery.

Moreover, it shows the ability, to quickly buy and sell subtle and obvious things.

And if need be, insert rumor or expose a closely guarded secret, to spark immediate notice and action by government and commercial interests, that includes the media, and especially "vigilant" outsiders. Or is the word "vigilante," or the Italian word *vigilia*, the eve of yet another conventional and unconventional war fund raiser promotion and/or special interest trade deal"?

***

However, a closer inspection of one computer screen gives the full impression of maps that could change the world.

As some have real-time aspects of map-based controllers, and things associated with control engineering, with guide open source higher-order functions that relate to the theory of categories and exceptions, bundle theory. And all seem more advance than Defense Advanced Research Projects Agency (DARPA), Darktrace, Homeland Security Advanced Research Projects Agency (HSARPA), Intelligence Advanced Research Projects Activity (IARPA), Defence Research and Development Canada, Tekes—the Finnish Funding Agency for Technology and Innovation—in addition to the Defence Science and Technology Organization, Defence Science and Technology Laboratory, Defence Research and Development Organisation, and the Defence Science and Technology Organisation.

In fact, the computer screens show real-time updates, of ultrasecret worldwide projects inside one exclusive research laboratory after another, and done so to maintain the niche system's fifty-year lead, ahead of the corporate-nation-state efforts, as collectively these outside projects reveal more than enough.

Especially as many internet providers, businesses, and governments seem fixated on petty disputes, such as step on an ant, another competitor, gender, team, tribe, nation, religion, and on yet another easy target of low hanging fruit, or something thought of as a weed, or an ant, the poor, or whatever?

***

In addition, the computer screens show each mission, design, function, content, timing, and so forth, such as strategic insider guides, each walkthrough, first mover advantage efforts, and prospector techniques.

Most importantly, all of these niche computer "physical systems" convey the full impression of a world power, a true superpower, a great hidden sovereign state of unparalleled influence on a global scale, and several advanced stages beyond that classic definition, and more than capable of delivering mutual assured destruction.

***

Moments later, this niche workstation deploys more elaborate short and long games, and does so with one ever so smooth technique after another.

Yet in total, one main function of the workstation is that of an if an ever-so-shrewd bookmaker, bookie, or turf accountant, who manipulates the betting line with specific techniques, that would amaze Michael de Montaigne, Jerome Cardan, René Descartes, John Montague, Fyodor Dostoevsky, Wild Bill Hickok—and especially Billy Walters.

And, on several computer screens, they seem to show weather maps that tract surface wind velocity, and by assigning a vector to each point on a map, and each vector represents the speed and direction air moves at that point.

Yet, a closer look at on one screen after another, a reoccurring theme appears.

These systems track various Lagrangian systems, field theory, field physics, gauge symmetry mathematics, of quantum field theory, and replacements of BRST symmetries, Faddeev–Popov gauge ghosts or Faddeev–Popov ghost fields, of extraneous introduced fields.

And, the term ghost has no relationship to a typical ghost, not a spooky being, although Albert Einstein used the term spooky referring to the alterity or entanglement, maybe part of the quantum entanglement system, a mostly hidden function of the universe.

Such as, an odd predicament or "necessity" that Albert Einstein, a German-born theoretical physicist, the theory of relativity, one of the two pillars of modern physics, mathematical objects, alongside quantum mechanics, described as a "spooky action at a distance." Of which, seems a bit vague for such an incredibly gifted person to have said, yet something another articulate scientist, musician or poet might better describe, a specialist, and with far more precision regarding all those obvious and subtle poetic aspects, especially when something seems mostly hidden, and beyond all conventional language and thought?

Instead, ghost refers to an outside field, force, unknown, or mystery, such as maybe a hidden overlay, underlay, and all points between ...

... or, the universal over- and under soul, and all points between ...

... or, the container and properties of, and how the container functions, such as poke here and it causes an effect elsewhere, such as step on a person's toe and that person's mouth says, "Ouch!" ...

... or some other person says, "Hey, why did you step on that person?"

In addition, gauge symmetry describes something within a system, and swappable language, such as different words, synonyms.

Whereas, a description of the same thing, in different languages, is called a duality, a dual nature, swappable, transpositional word, phrase, thing, and/or function; something that exists in another language(s), system(s), field(s) within a bundle theory technique.

And these computer screens show these as a map and compelling rulebook of fields, of those swappable per other systems.

***

Or say another way, some of these computer screens seem as if real-time maps that monitor and/or manipulate security prices, finances, currencies exchanges, interest rates, bundles of, and flow, quantity, quality, and much, much more.

***

Yet from this vantage point, it seems quite difficult to accurately describe most of the system functions in great detail.

***

Then moments later, material shown on one screen after another encrypt, with a post-quantum cryptography technique, a three supersingular isogeny graphs with the same vertex set, yet different edge sets, a "cryptographic hash function that contains: start from a fixed vertex, of a supersingular isogeny graph, with bits of binary representation from an input value, to regulate a sequence of edges that track in a walk of the graph, and uses identity of the vertex reached at the walks end, as the hash value for the input."

And, seems to do so because there are no known subexponential-time methods to break this scheme, not even on a quantum computer.

▼

PART 8

Then moments later, at that crowd Manhattan accident, around a dead Will Ferrell, aka David, and *Erika Segersäll Unræd*, the Scandinavian, unusual air swirls, and again, then smells of sycamore, birch, and mulberry.

***

And inside this niche, at the heavily fortified vacant workstation, it seems to have other functions, as if a station port, reference stream, reference point indentation, permanent dwell, and a place for demarcation transactions, such as the process to start and end a transaction, that uses begin, commit, and rollback methods.

And, that workstation has an aspect to stand guard and not go beyond, as if it has something to do with structural and territorial integrity with a separation of powers.

And, in back of the workstation, a few steps outside that sphere of influence, it leads to a poorly lit narrow path that has a tremendous pull into.

***

So much so, and off to the left side, several weak beings desperately warn away from that path, wave off, and again, then strain to breathe.

And these "creatures," for lack of a better description, seem transhuman or posthuman, with colorful, irresistible, and creepy gravitas, such as slowly back away from them, with no sudden moves. As some of them use Fluorinert, an experimental liquid breathing system and coolant based on stable fluorocarbon fluid.

And two of the transhumans or posthumans have the endocranial anatomy more similar to Dwykaselachus and Callorhinchus milii, yet vastly improved mental capacities and evolved functions, and beyond traditional human brain components.

HUMAN BRAIN

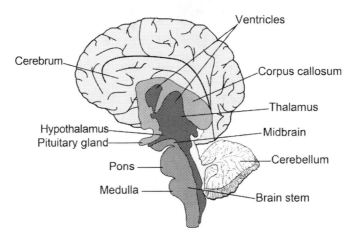

Especially, as those creatures seem quite interesting, as compared to a human brain, the medulla, pons, cerebellum, midbrain, diencephalon, and the telencephalon expanse …

… that last great human evolutionary trait …

… that major system distortion, as if an overgrowth, a bulge, opportunity, port, physical transport layer, and implications …

… of what the telencephalon expanse system will, and will not allow.

CHAPTER 42

▼

PART 9

And compared to, what another brain aspects could offer, if allowed that same expansion opportunity and preferential treatment as the telencephalon expanse, such as special insider privileges, a great transformation.

And the xenophobe says to self, "Humans seem to have a very slow maturation rate, such as ever so slow learners, poor focus, impulsive, obsessive, obtuse, stubborn, quite foolish, and often determine to follow so many masters at the same time, such as gender, family, friends, tribe, team, employer, economic system, politic, cult, religion, and race, such as an endless race.

"And, how does a person survive among all these powerful masters, of all expected devotion, to yet another fault?

***

"And on average, humans gravitate towards drama, vice, and fixation, that often includes gossip, energy drinks, starches, cigarettes, chocolates, clothing, shoes, pet rocks, and other impulse behavior.

"And, that includes shopping on an empty stomach, overspending, in denial, poor quality drinking water, then fast food, to name a few.

***

"And, as a baseline, they prefer a stereotype, a bias, and what a system expects, to pander on cue, as if a quick-change artist into a fault; and often into a trope, a stereotype, or typical bias; such as the forty to fifty common cognitive biases, as one loyalty test after another, that often creates a strange reality.

✻✻✻

"And, the system is not loyal to the members, as members seem quite disposable, often told so then proved time and time again, and the members know this.

"And often, the system maneuvers members to vote for this disposable philosophy, that strange phenomenon, to mostly vote against oneself, tighten that trap, often creating a strange reality with odd contradicting rules, and yet another justification?

✻✻✻

"And exactly, what have humans been doing for the last 200,000 years or so, and that chain of events.

"Was most of the time spent searching for another common grubstake; for example, the history of the human species, and the universe in general, of yet another below average quality grubstake, sold at an above average price, and that 200,000 years or so chain of events.

"Such as, a person must fully subscribe to, an enemy-of-the-month club, then qualify for a below-average quality grubstake, at an above-average price, that often requires a long-term payment plan?"

▼

PART 10

And, in back of the workstation, a few steps outside that sphere of influence, it leads to a poorly lit narrow path then tunnel that has a tremendous pull into.

***

So much so, and again, those severely weak transhumans or posthumans, with colorful, irresistible, and creepy gravitas desperately wave off any attempt to touch things in this niche, especially enter that path.

And, they do so again, then strain to breathe.

***

As before, they warned other people, who entered this niche, explored, then received a tremendous equipment shock that reduced them into an ugly feeble, a person who mostly slumps, drools, and mumbles, then once in a while, has a wild-eye-fully-animate notion.

And as a result, these previous trespassers could not articulate a clear line of effort, and each new attempt, to articulate caused them very active and colorful delirium, then gestic hallucinations, delusions, disorganizations and confusions about preposition, postposition, and circumposition.

Then, the articulation slowed to muddled speech, about a very complex subject, about the next great zeitgeist or major breakthru, such as a major mystery, an unsolved problem in physics, mathematics, chemistry, biology, medicine, or about Ramanujan's lost notebook, Ludwig Wittgenstein's notebooks, or third-culture kid, equilibrium techniques, or leaky mathematical abstractions.

And, as the vital revelation neared, that person reached a great mental barrier, realized it then ranted with wild-eyed delirium at the wilderness, at the frontier, and trapped in that endless cycle, of a person kept as a garden vegetable, a trial garden, or much worst.

So, avoid this niche and tunnel system.

CHAPTER 42

▼

PART 11

PUBLISHER NOTE: A CHAPTER COMPONENT,
DELIBERATELY WITHHELD BY THE WRITER

CHAPTER 42

▼

PART 12

And, in back of that niche workstation, three steps away, outside the sphere of influence, it leads to that poorly lit, narrow path, with tremendous pull into a tunnel like no other, such as thru one stage after another, surrounded by walls and ceiling that contain dense layers of bizarre *Wunderkammer*, *Leverian, façade* style, and something an articulate scientist, musician, or *aristo* poet may better describe with far more precision, regarding all those obvious and subtle aspects.

***

As that tremendous force pulls in, space greatly narrows, feels ever so tight, then compressed from one outer containment process or function after another.

Of which, it pulls into one exceptionally complex route then routes, multifaceted, individual complex states with tremendous forces, unusual patterns, more options, isolated bits, pieces, points, concepts, references, space, other realities quite difficult to describe, some temporal, and others seems to transcend all conventional language and thought.

***

And along the way, the pull increases.

As a result, and often, along that path, to avoid serious damage or worse, a person must make one ultraquick twitch decision then one maneuver after another, sometimes exceptionally subtle, while other times quite awkward or inexcusably strange, weird, or objectionable under normal circumstances, especially if seen in a social setting.

Yet here, any part of the body could touch a tunnel system aspect, mostly hidden, and it would have very serious implications, often quick, yet maybe minutes, hours, days, months, or years later, such as inescapable.

***

And along that path, a person must quickly choose an idea, concept, philosophy, system, yet eventually betray, then land on one series of unusual stepping stones after another, or one substantial place after another.

As if each stone or place serves a complex algebraic function, such as a pan-national epic, complex function, z-plane, *sui generis*, then full grip of collective identity, a conditional gene knockout, yet often more.

And, a person needs to avoid stepping into a wrong moment, or situation that disables a person's true potential, or worse yet, makes "feeble," of all known definitions.

***

In addition, this paths and/or transportation technique seems as if an experiment of pure science, to predict, manage, locate natural phenomena, and hidden resources, based on empirical evidence from observation and experimentation, especially control techniques of the "hidden universal empire" if you will.

As most of it and the universe, functions, abilities, and locations remain unknown.

***

And, along these paths and most endpoints, so many odd things and reality exist, often loops, a functional iteration, mostly into yet another form of harsh poverty, a bounded function, and others much worse, such as a literal or figurative hellhole, a "same-old, same-old" serious dysfunction, of yet another misadventure, less freedom, and high stress in a classic "quagmire" or "trap" in every sense of those two words.

So much so, a tunnel system and most endpoints, seem as if rules often shift, seem heavily gerrymandered against public and private reasonable, then accurate long-term memory, a history of ideas and effectiveness; as if a "rigged experiment," system, quagmire, trap with powerful and meticulous bias against a paradise forming, a golden age of peace, such as age, *saeculum*, or *aeon*.

***

And, in that respect, it functions quite similar to the universe, a bias against paradise.

***

So much so, it seems as if the niche system and universe in general are desperately in search of something.

***

And, in this niche tunnel system, endpoints, and universe in general, it also seems as if a desperate search for reliable ways or means, to easily implement a system, a "reliable set of ultimate, discrete universal unfolding techniques, rules, norms, and laws."

Yet for people who trespass, all people do so direct or indirectly, the niche and universe deliberately maintains a very specific mental fog, atmospheric, state, hyper and, yet another distraction, as it relates to solving substantial problems, especially from locating a reliable exit, from any given quagmire.

***

Or say another way, it seems as if, most aspects of this niche and tunnel system remains hidden and elsewhere, the alterity, entanglement, maybe part of the quantum entanglement system, and the "mythology of lost" based on real science.

Of equal or greater importance, it seems this place, and especially the universe is rigged …

… probably a built-in back-formation technique …

... from rigging, to fit an idea, situation or ship with rigging ...

... to clothe with special gear, into a condition or position for use, as if to preposition, adjust, arrange, a truly great ship ...

... rigged for something, a function, a construct for manual control, yet in effect, one ever so temporary shelter after another, such as shelter from the last and present storm.

***

Or say another way, and possibly, a better visualization, the overall niche tunnel system shape resembles an "ultimate analytic extension," a complex function not quite, as per Dmitrii Kouznetosv, or analytic extension of the Ackermann function, with exceptionally complex routes, multifaceted, and tremendous forces, unusual patterns, options, isolated bits, I, space, time, other things quite difficult to describe, and many mislead or distract from vital issues.

As, the niche tunnel paths often lead to one path after another, an isolated idea, step, position, remote position, or island.

And often, regarding any of these positions, to the left and right is a literal or figurative hellhole, such as, once in a literal or figurative hellhole, often poverty or worst, it seems best to escape, regardless of the local agreements, contracts, laws to stay, submit, and serve.

So, ever so discreetly escape without a ripple.

And, many niche places, seem as if an endlessly loop.

And, some paths seem as if a complex circle, yet ultimately arrive at bizarre, or truly bizarre.

For example, many things inside the paths seem quite risky, such as a person may touch the wrong idea or place, then is pushed into a loop that seems as if, yet another endless mission drift.

Such as, it starts as a great idea, belief system, project, then mission drift, into yet another quagmire with tremendous, tenacious gravitas.

***

And, some things inside the niche and paths feel, as if deliberately made complex, asymmetrical bias, of deliberate symmetry violations in a physical and abstract way, such as the literal and figurative ways then means.

In fact, many paths seem as if hidden categories, with so many biases, especially formed at the universal beginning, the big bang of "baby you know me," a best-design effort on a bad day, to start a new system, or a universe.

***

And, just as importantly, regarding the niche system, as strange as it may seem, all paths and things inside the paths ultimately seem correct in their own right, yet most seem incorrect in relationship to each other.

***

And, to a conventional mindset or perspective, the entire path process seems quite bizarre, lacks logic, such as inductive, abductive, deductive.

And, it defies common sense, in a way that feels quite dangerous, and often, as if much of the universe seems 50/50, random, or arbitrary, and depends on individual discretion, on that vast multitude of distributives.

***

As a result of all these things, inside this niche tunnel system, and along the way, pass one sinister place after another, it floods the mind with so many different emotions, and too many to list, such as squeamishness.

Then lips tremble, and that person feels serious regret as warm tears flow, then face shows tremendous suffering, as if true pathos quite difficult to describe, then a brief joy, followed by awe at the entire process.

And that cycle continues in very distinct stages that eventually exhaust the mind, body, and soul.

***

And, a few of these paths lead to a number of unusual places quite difficult to fully describe, such as some similarities to Konark Sun Temple, thirteenth-century, India, yet built of supreme dense technocracy with the finest detail.

And this place sits in a location similar to the Zhangjiajie National Forest Park, Hunan Province, China.

Yet more unusual than that, this temple's surrounding location also contains features similar to four other places that include Salar de Uyuni, Bolivia, and unusual polygonal fractures in sandstones, similar to a Jurassic outcrop at Grand Staircase-Escalante National Monument, bizarre rock formations in Cappadocia, Turkey, and Hoodoos formations in Bryce Canyon National Park, Inspiration Point, Utah, USA.

And, near that temple are bizarre rock formations similar to the Kent Mountains, Kazakhstan, with an outcrop that has a very unusual eternal flame, a natural phenomenon produced by a natural gas leak, peat fire, coal seam fire, or an eternal object/particle/thing/an it, that burns as if for an eon or more.

And not far away, attached to yet slightly receded into the main temple wall, facing this unusual eternal flame unique activity, a source of light, heat and power, especially warm sunlight, is a throne, "the Nth Degree."

***

So much so, it reveals a certain truth, beauty, and mysterious beams of completeness, of totality; a peaceful majestic glory, as if a fully realized redemption, and the source, to support a great culture.

And, this structure seems as if the source of a truly great civilization, and corresponds with the throne and mind of who would sits there, as exceptional mental vapors rise, the atmospherics, and ethereal vivid universal dream of a psychonautic, that sails through distinguished states, properties, and *sui generis sae* fresh, and fair.

***

And, this throne has a special heavily ornate design, as if a category persistent cradle-to-cradle system.

And, it seems especially designed for an outcast, someone rejected by society, such as similar to the public meeting practice in Ancient Athenian Greece, of writing "a person's name on a shard of broken pottery," that metaphor, then placing it in a large container, counting the results, then if a sufficient number exists, the person was banished for ten years.

Yet in this case, as if eternal, an infinite duration, for this "hero with a thousand faces," and someone not related to Mitochondrial Eve, or last tribe of, or tribes, of all currently living humans, and as if the original government in exile.

***

And, this throne is a place to rest, really rest, and recover from the original event.

Yes, and relax.

Yes.

Breathe.

Yes.

Really breathe, and lay back.

Yes.

Relax, really relax on a supreme pillow, the best of the best.

***

And, if need be, consider the message and thematics of "Sheryl Crow - Long Way Back?" an official audio.

CHAPTER 42

▼

PART 13

And, a closer look at this throne gives the full impression of unquestionable glory, with the imperial quality of Napoleon, Imperial Senate throne of Pedro II of Brazil, and a secular version of the superstructure glory behind the chair of Saint Peter, Saint Peter's Basilica, Rome; that golden luminous event of mega, for lack of a more accurate description, such as something beyond description.

***

And this throne seems as if the "Nth Degree," a fully functional secular system and with exceptional aesthetics, that deploys the science of a supreme technocracy and all that greatness of effective scientific innovation, with a universal applicability of the scientific method, a true meritocracy, a superior unlimited system.

And of equal importance, this throne gives the full impression of an official residence, with a fortified, fully functional crown system, not populated with trinkets, or jewels, whether flawed, midland, or supreme, yet populated with indescribable things…

..., surpass description and ever so shrewd juggernauts, of small enough to fit on the crown, and various-size supreme beings, of tribe, village, town, city, city-state, quite substantial yet ever last, a vital eon, universal, with a blank verse ability, metrical writing system.

And throughout the crown system, it has a dactylic hexameter, as if the epic verse of classical times, also called a heroic meter, and iambic pentameter heroic line, with a universal bit, a plow, to cut, lift, and turn over soil, both literal or metaphorical, as if it chronicles the universe from pre-big until now.

In addition, this crown and throne system seems older that dirt, the Iron Age, Bronze Age, Great Apes, likely older than an eon, older than the universe, a beach-size thing.

***

Such as, two, three, four!

CHAPTER 42

▼

PART 14, A

And this crown has no laurel wreath components made of flowers, oak leaves, or thorns, such as place on the head, then quench an extreme thirst with vinegar, as a prize, based on yet another *coup d'état* over reasonable, another *coup d'essai*, or *coup de theatre*, as in *stratégie de la corde raide*, or English land law and Law of Property Act 1925, to gain yet again, a decisive victory of one good shot—a third act.

It seems to be the original purpose of a crown, the first version that humans often mimic since Mitochondrial Eve, or last tribe of, or tribes, of all currently living humans.

As it is a fully functional, practical, efficient, effective system, the best of the best, a true glory, much of it alive, and quite capable.

It is not similar to the Vajracarya's Ritual Crown, Ancient Nepal, Crown of the Essen Cathedral Treasury, Crown of the Holy Roman Empire, crown of King Christian IV of Denmark, Crown of Saint Wenceslas, Russian tsar's crown, Imperial Crown of Russia, or Imperial Crown of Napoleon III of France.

Yet it has some similar features to the Kingdom of Nepal Imperial Crown's Head of the States and Ancient Nepal Vajracarya's Ritual Crown, however much more spectacular, and not populated with trinkets, or jewels, whether flawed, midland, or supreme.

It is populated by a considerable number of supreme beings, a coalition of.

That also seems as if universal and biological theater, a considerable microcosm, an experimental ecosystem, and those dynamics to sustain

171

in some form of symbiosis, a set of persistent biological interactions maybe mutualistic, commensalistic, parasitic, with superregnum archaea, superregnum bacteria, superregnum eukaryota regnum protista, regnum fungi, regnum plantae, regnum animalia, virus, yet mostly beings, machines, and ever so potent synthetic life.

And, this complex microcosm contains communities, agents, and world with worlds that flourish, the best of the best, self-assembling supreme technocracy of an open system, and other things quite difficult to accurately describe, yet seem as if a trial garden.

***

And, next to this throne, within reach are a few highly organized, fully indexed spectacular scepters, ornamental staffs, wands, ceremonial weapons, such as a similar style of the gold *ruyi* with carved flowers, Qing dynasty, Palace Museum, yet all have living components, vital functioning abilities, world with worlds, and no cheap symbolics, or classic bejeweled.

And these spectacular scepters, ornamental staffs, wands, ceremonial weapons are not fake, imitations, a great pretender, as most commercialism is fake, yet another gross exaggeration, often plastic, a wannabe, that often imitates, as a copy of a copy, and not original content.

And some of these things have various special meiotic functions, tools to monitor meromorphic events and ontology, branch management, frames of reference, and manifolds in topological space, especially positions of guided open source higher-order functions, and multiple socket.io addresses, domains, and various outlets.

As if some of these things are a superordinate principal, a universal chess master, a superus, conditional of *superi*, that skill, that ability to utilize a superior understanding of strategy, and with the ability to monitor activity in folded space, a complex manifold system, a state within a state, the deep state. And do so as if the universe is a manifold, or every point in the universe governs a localizing manifold system.

And some, especially the scepters, ornamental staffs, and wands have a complex multilateral chiasma linguistic function real time, with a unique tonal adjustment ability, as if a universal prosodic translator, with simultaneous functions.

And each seems to exist partially out of phase, as if partially cloaked, or invisible matter, or dark matter, for example, possibly an aspect of supra and/or subspace, as in some integral part and nuisance location within spacetime; of one distinct and yet coexistent with normal space.

And some, especially the scepters, ornamental staffs, and wands have an ability to project action, a subtle, mid or gross narrow beam of energy that generates facticity or thrownness, especially temporal thrownness, disorientation, and the ability to monitor and manage a threshold event, especially a mid-ritual event. Such as, after a person or thing exits the original state of identity, time, and community; that process.

So much so, each scepter, ornamental staff, and wand seems to have the ability to manage suprachiasmatic, a body's circadian rhythms, while another device settings create a delta wave feel that may affect or modify the thalamus.

All and all, the recession into the main temple wall, that contains the throne system, crown, scepters, ornamental staffs, wands, ceremonial weapons give the full impression of tremendous power, legitimacy, victory, triumph, honor, and glory, as if as immortality, righteousness, and resurrection, to "the Nth Degree."

***

And, most of this throne's physical system seems alive, though not in that classic sense of life, not a carbon-based life form.

As carbon represents the key component within all known life on Earth, natural life that is.

Such as, how does a living thing fix carbon, a tetravalent?

And, this throne has a human aspect, as if an evolutionary extension of the mind.

Such as, the way something may eventually overcome the human brain's structural disadvantages, of originating from a savage species, *ferae naturae*, that primitive structural and related legacy baggage, and biota coalition, within an empire of self; the skittish, jealous, and pettifog within. That often impulses a bitter shout at one minor problem after another, or shout at the devil, or some other cultural equivalent, and often as a distraction because of procrastination regarding the near and dear issues of self.

Especially, and often, humans make a "devil" for profit, or some other cultural equivalent; as yet another commercial or political fund raiser.

Such as, someone, tribe, or coalition of, deliberately herds crime and war refugees into a peaceful community, often into a wealthy community, for example Scandinavia. As yet another petty ways and means to make a profit, a make work program, or a public or private works program, "a shovel-ready project." Yet often profits channel into yet another narrow interest, or to prop up a tribe, coalition of, industry or entire economy; yet often a war-of-the-month club that systematically removes money, freedom of speech, and draws more people into; the same old remote 5,000-or-so-year-old or more tribal dispute.

A dispute that long ago started, because of one very bad marriage, or series of.

And, all their tribes originate from a very bad marriage, and on occasion made worse, mated with very attractive nontribal concubines, or male equivalent?

Or marriage, at a critical lineage juncture, between a tribal member and nontribal member; mate with an original, an exceptionally smart, mentally agilic principal, a very stubborn aesthetic, a true artist, artistic, not caught up in a classic, long standing tribal dispute, compressed linear chained knots, buffers and chain couplers of that tribe and related tribes.

Such as, a 5,000-year-or -so -old tribe, or related tribes, long ago mated with an unusual, and the effects move thru their lineage.

***

Hence, the tribal rule, never marry outside the tribe or tribes, as it will create offspring quite smart yet obsessive, hypersensitive, prone to hype yet again, to a fault; and often say urgent, then cry wolf.

***

So nowadays, much of the world suffers because of that original tribe mistake?

***

And if we do not agree, they use slight, mid and gross ways and means, to make it so.

***

And, say their collective name, and they swarm.

And often, the powers-that-be use a new age computerized media technique, a vinculum, or some may say a thinkculum, yet a more accurate word and/or phrase has been deliberately removed from this book series and previous book series.

One that more accurately summarizes a system technique, that formulates precise daily media scripts and talking points, that adjusts daily, with a new formulated twist, something extra, a little something here, and a little there to keep things "fresh"—well, fresher—and with a very specific protocol.

Or, inserting "stale" maybe the better word.

Such as, deliberately inserting something quite stale, the same old tribal 5,000-or-so-year-old or more disputed, when a vital freshness is needed, at a critical moment, and again.

Exploits human vulnerabilities, again.

That classic technique.

To deliberately keep humans quite vulnerable.

Yet often, into the mass media stream, that system deliberately inserts, "rot, filth, and divisiveness."

And occasionally, deploys things from the controversial stockpiles of software and hardware vulnerabilities, especially during the fundraising season, that each time seems longer, and longer.

And that system uses a tried and true method, similar to what drug addicts seek, not any old stack.

They seek the elusive quintessential protocol stack.

However, this technique, often seems quite fake, and gives a simple lazy tweet or whatever, that ability to spark visceral excitement, buzz, impulse, urgent, and shallow tenacious clamor for, yet another high-stakes gamble.

And based on historical divisiveness, yet not enough to truly reform the system, mostly offer a classic grubstake; as they mimic, the original bad marriage, and shift aspects of the quagmire for quick profit, such as that endless yin and yang chase of who is right, and wrong, then that system says, "We Didn't Start the Fire."

✳✳✳

Yet, follow the money, that trail of profits, especially common size results, to find the big financial winners.

As, the thinkculum rallies forces by all means necessary.

And, it especially uses divisive issues, wedge issues, and things exceptionally difficult to stand on without experiencing danger, or places difficult to sit in, or think about for very long, let alone have a comprehensive and objective debate.

For instance, in this brave new Orwellian world, it often promotes shouting at the "cash cows," for lack of a better phrase.

Such as, an idea, philosophy, person and/or system on the enemy-of-the-month club list.

Or shout at the new-age indentured servants, shout at this stark, cruel, and miserable expanse, of people slowly sinking into poverty, such as a modern version of the poorhouse.

And shout at those most vulnerable, who greatly suffer, as if they made the constitution, write laws, and have tremendous power, plus true economic mobility.

Drug tests school children, mothers on welfare, and modern wage slaves, yet not the seniormost leaders of corporations, governments, churches, and massive nonprofits with tremendous power, wealth, and control over the world economy, the rudder and control of too big to fail, of tremendous systemic risk from a massive concentration of treasure, such as into a narrower, and narrower group; that magnification, that leverage.

Such as, avoid too much sun, especially magnification, as it can quickly crisp a vital point.

Or, think of it another way, leverage works both ways, for and against, especially tremendous leverage, a tremendous concentration of power.

Or, chase these seniormost leaders, as a fan: fandom, and those inflated costs?

So much so, a phenomenon may occur, diminishing returns, physics: push a sting.

And one mistake by anyone of these members of an ever so narrowing group, or tainted by something, prejudice, error, and/or corruption, and the damage could quickly create an ever so dangerous chain systemic reaction, worldwide?

And yet, worldwide systems concentrate more and more power into this main economic control center and engine technique, and into one very skittish financial district after another.

And in a moment's notice, anywhere along this string or chain, they risk a panic, dump, and run event.

Yet, for the expendables, the average person, those complex obligations, especially debt remain tenaciously attached to them, and they have no significant financial liquidity or escape options.

And in part, by design, these financial markets, and people in general, are heavily conditioned by the education system, and especially the media, with one misinformation technique after another, with classic hype, exaggerations, fantasy, commercialism, and propaganda that is often total nonsense, sold as the new norm; yet sold when the system and people need vital sustenance, at one strategic moment after another.

That makes the collective more susceptible to gossip and panic, especially the financial markets, filled with very skittish people, who control the world economy?

So, financial markets, in a moment's notice, can and often based on a rumor or fake news by competition, withdraw critical, financial support, then, in a split second, move massive amounts of capital out, such as, can quickly drain an entire company, village, town, and/or city employer, and that systemic risk.

Then, of that ever so narrowing group, seniormost leaders can press an app, for very good reasons, legally transfer massive wealth out, then legally and seamlessly escape.

Really escape, if need be, to some far-off place, a paradise, *paradiso*, maybe a perennial Neoplatonism, NeoScandinavian, or official transcendent paradise, with really good water, such as in a Gan Eden, Avalon, Baltia, Shambhala, Beyul, El Dorado, or *Stabiae*, a very long vacation, new home, yet a historical place, famous, with magnificent Roman style villas, or some other cultural equivalent.

Or, go to a place known for excellent water, such as what was loosely described, in *The Travels of Sir John Mandeville*, or by Juan Ponce de León, the snapback effect of vitality-restoring waters.

And that cool sip, which redeems and restores original intent, aspiration, and reserve of spark.

Or, sip water under a tree of life, of knowledge, or a localized version, a one-of-a-kind, an idiosyncratic.

Or, sip exceptional water, in one of the top twenty hideaways for the superrich, or yet another tax haven.

Yet do not take a "vacation express," such as, a person needs the change of pace, change of scenery, a real and substantial vacation, conspicuous leisure, conspicuous consumption, spending money on, and acquiring luxury goods and services, and not a quick rest or getaway, not a pit stop, or three-day weekend.

As mostly, a "vacation express" consists of planning, shopping for, packing, traveling thru airport traffic, hurry and mostly wait here and there, such as in the airport, shuffling in that stark regimental system, grumbling, shuffling to a seat, looking for luggage overhead storage, listening to a passenger have a very-loud-ever-so-personal-and-frivolous-last-minute cell phone call, sitting in a tight seat with poor leg room, listening to loud common sense airplane announcements about safety, waddling out of the plane, waiting for bags, traveling thru airport traffic, arriving at hotel, unpacking, depressurizing, paying high tourist rates for below-average

BRYAN FLETCHER

results, preparing to leave, packing, traveling thru airport traffic, waiting in the airport, shuffling in that stark regimental system, grumbling, shuffling to a seat, looking for luggage overhead storage, listening to a passenger have a very-loud-ever-so-personal-and-frivolous-last-minute cell phone call, sitting in a tight seat with poor leg room, listening to loud common sense airplane announcements about safety, waddling out of the plane, waiting for bags, traveling thru airport traffic, arriving home, unpacking, and remembering all those things.

And, as a person grogs.

Feels sleepy, and again.

Often, the head suddenly nods with a hypnic jerk, a sleep-start-event; a sudden major involuntary jolt that startles a person, with the shock from falling, such as into a great void.

***

Yet each time, regarding the heavy sleep impulse, the person fully denies; that pattern.

***

However, to sleep, the person eventually surrenders, and rests head on a cool, comfy 100% cotton pillow.

***

Yet soon, memories of that "hurry and mostly wait classic vacation express" replay in the mind, such as would of, could of, should of, and did, in one scenario after another.

***

Yet, to an equal or great concern, a seniormost corporate leaders, government, church, and massive nonprofits with tremendous power, wealth, and control over the world economy may escape to conspicuous leisure, conspicuous consumption, such as Marina di Portofino, Italy, Cote d'Azur, France, St. Barthélemy, Caribbean, Ibiza, Spain, Davos, Switzerland, or the Maldives.

Or escape, and buy an island retreat, for instance Northern Aegean, or Omfori Island, Greece.

Or find, an equivalent of, maybe better; *Stabiae*, a vacation, historical place, famous, with magnificent Roman style villas, or some other cultural equivalent, of conspicuous leisure, conspicuous consumption.

Then, wait for the economic turmoil to settle.

And, wait there as a gentleman, or gentlewoman, maybe as a framer, or farmer, or hobby gardener.

Or, live there as yet another literal and metaphorical trial garden.

Or buy Mouchão de Alhandra Island in Portugal, or buy Venice Island, Italy, Mermaid Isle, Ireland, Kings Island, Denmark, or Stora Rullingen, Sweden.

Or, well, in this brave new world, a person is rich, yet cash-poor, and must function on a tight budget, quite so, then consider buying Hangover Island, Florida, Leader Island, Nova Scotia, Mannions, or Staff Island, Ireland, Ofu Island, Tonga, or Mavuva Island, Fiji.

Or, consider buying Flannan Isles, Outer Hebrides, or Bouvet Island, that is an island located at the southern end of the Mid-Atlantic Ridge, and maybe find a place near Nyrøysa, or some other part of the world, warmer, such as live in a sacred bamboo forest.

As, many of these elite people, seem more than capable of a quickly exit...

... the senior most corporate leaders, government, church, and massive nonprofits with tremendous power, wealth, and control over the world economy...

... the rudder and control of too big to fail, of tremendous systemic risk from a massive concentration treasure, again, that pattern; a super cycle, that needs vital substance, ever so smooth, circumspection, proper timing, piquancy, a lively arch charm and permanence.

***

Yes.
Yes.
And, yes.

***

Ride it out in a paradise.

For example, live in a tropical paradise retreat, and sip a fancy drink, a colada, maybe a pina colada, passion, or guava, the colorful, with a tiny umbrella.

Or, drink a classic colorful strawberry daiquiri, banana, watermelon, or mint.

Or, a person can sip a fine wine, a special treat, French, of course— bright, warm, and sophisticated.

And, pour in a very particular way.

Then, take a passive wine inhalation, and another, that resembles a quick series of sniffs, followed by a pause, serious consideration, then one long gentle sniff.

Next, use active inhalation, that uses both mouth and nose, with a glass tilted forty degrees towards a person, then head leans toward a glass, with nose just above the glass and mouth open a quarter of an inch—where, through the mouth and nose, a gentle breathe in and out captures, then measures, one wine note after another, as well as other vital nuances.

***

Then, meticulously inspect the wine for clarity, brightness, rim variation, primary and secondary color...

... sediment and particle size.

***

Then sip, measure, realize the best of old world charm.

***

If so, maybe, it causes a person to spark, delight, gush, buzz, and chat about this wine, a bright future, so much so, on this island, continue, and build a spectacular mansion retreat, as tribute.

Or, sip on a single malt whisky special, neat, an exceptionally educated sustenance, a masterpiece, with sufficient pure spirit, from each simple distillation "stage," in every sense of the word, to make a cleaner, an ever so lighter spirit, of two-wash, four spirits, from wash, feint, spirit, fore shot, dud run, wee witchee, and the heart.

Made from exceptional water of a secret Scandinavian spring, or some other exceptional source; from Rowan Tree Burn, the Scurran Burn, or the Benrinnes Spring?

Regardless, the whisky has considerable gravitas, an ever so smooth flavor then lifting spirit threshold, with sophistication, such as a masterpiece, and what one expects at an elite event, such as the Pebble Beach *Concours d'Elegance.*

Then, sip again, and complain about departed glories, the way it was in the good old days, in yesteryear, before the others ruined it.

And do so until the Federal Reserve, another central bank, or quite likely, a political wantabe calls, and offers a very special return home invitation, a personal invitation, such as a huge near-zero interest rate loan, or negative rates, and/or a ten-year real estate tax abatement, or some other treat that shifts the burden elsewhere.

Of which, these have become the new methods to lure this very special crowd, lure them home.

Back into this ultimate insider circle, and that chase, that courtship, as well as offer an elite form of salary and perks, as if fandom.

Of which, can put an economic system, more and more under the control of fewer and fewer people, the financial districts and proxies of, many of whom are skittish for both good and bad reasons, and fair weather friends?

Some of these people may say, 'We Didn't Start the Fire.'

***

Yet, follow the money, that trail of profits, especially the big financial winners, of making a systemic "devil" for profit, or some other cultural equivalent; as if yet another commercial or political fundraiser.

The thinkculum rallies forces by all means necessary.

And, it especially promotes divisive issues, wedge issues, figurative red meat for the constituent base, yet bitterness to the opposition.

And things exceptionally difficult to speak of, without experiencing acute danger.

Or places difficult to sit in, or think about, let alone have a reasonable, comprehensive, and objective peer-reviewable debate, then full long-term satiable reconciliation.

In the media, on average, it promotes everyone, to join the war of the month club, and those expensive monthly membership fees, for below-average results.

Yet lately, it promotes dozens and dozens of daily kinetic and cultural wars, especially against the usual subjects, the usual trek, with people clearly marked with a classic cultural symbol, a logo, icon, uniform, or wearing certain colors, to denote and connote loyalty, and maybe wear a trope, such as a blue, gold, mauve, or red shirt.

Yet, no one in his or her right mind wants to be a redshirt trope, a disposable, treated as a vast number of people are, as suspects, such as an entire network of family, friend, tribe, team, employer, town, politic, culture, religion, race, gender or other social constructs.

Or worse yet, treats them as a thing, an animal, filthy savage, or an it, and does so over and over.

Then the system truly shocks when a percent of them radicalize from all that enormous pressure, and become the enemy. Of which it seems, a lesson, the powers rarely learned. Or, they deliberately do so, as yet another sly fund-raising technique, to earn a few coins, such as betray the golden age of peace, betray the concept of Jesus, or some other cultural variation, a universal principle of, a truly civilized system, in Europe, Asia, Americas, Oceania, and other island bits, many with a fresh cool whispery breeze.

※※※

Yet here and now, of equal or greater importance, this throne system is none of that, none of that divisiveness, wedge issues, sly fund-raising technique to earn a few coins, of make a "devil" for profit, classic hype, exaggeration, fantasy, commercialism, and propaganda that is often total nonsense, yet sold as the new norm.

▼

PART 14, B

Again, this throne system seems partly human, as if an evolutionary extension of the mind.

Such as, the way something may eventually overcome the human brain's structural disadvantages, of originating from a savage species, *ferae naturae*, that primitive structural and related legacy baggage, and biota coalition, within an empire of self; the skittish, jealous, and pettifog within. That often impulses a bitter shout at one minor problem after another, or shout at the devil, or some other cultural equivalent, and often as a distraction because of procrastination regarding the near and dear issues of self.

Especially as the social systems, often seem quite stuck, such as in the last literal and/or metaphorical war(s).

Especially, a make work program, make a "devil" for profit, or some other cultural equivalent; as yet another commercial, political fund-raiser, or petty dispute, such as someone, tribe, or coalition of, deliberately herds kinetic and cultural war refugees into a peaceful community, and at times into a wealthy community, for example Scandinavia.

❖❖❖

And, of equal or greater importance, regarding this throne system, a closer, and closer look, shows each new major developmental stage of mind, body, soul, and atmospherics, especially major improvements of traditional human brain components, that include the medulla, pons, cerebellum, midbrain, diencephalon, and the telencephalon expanse, that last great evolutional effort, that major system distortion, as if an overgrowth, a bulge, opportunity, port, and physical transport layer.

HUMAN BRAIN

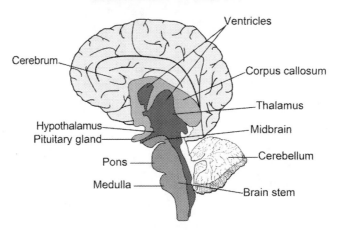

With implications of what the telencephalon expanse system will and will not allow, as compared to what another brain components may offer, if allowed that same opportunity, of a great distortion, as if a major overgrowth, a bulge.

In addition, this throne in exile shows each new brain component expansion and supplements, the what if, in a considerable number of brain segments, major improvements in organic components, regions, and natural barriers.

And, this throne does so to create a large, fortified, and detachable aspects of the new body, mind, and soul.

Such as all those systems, tools, devices, and beings that support an extraordinary encephalization quotient and query skills of a resourceful, penetrating, and definitive wit, as implied in *The Nth Degree, Star Trek, The Next Generation* with Lt. Reginald Barclay, though this throne system is no holographic interface.

▼

PART 15

Moments later, in back of this throne, and thru a center chamber that leads from an *enfilade* system, a toddler emerges, and waddles about the throne systems, a bundle theory, and all the while points with a right index finger at one elaborate throne feature after another, and each time, says things in a toddler language.

Of which, most people would not understand.

Yet if there, other toddlers would hear, notice, and some would nod yes, as if a good understanding of "toddlerism," distinctive gestures, vocabulary, and philosophy; a pre-formal education system perspective, pre-indoctrination, before the harsh regimental system humans demand, gravitate to, and support as if the Holy Grail, or some other religious system equivalent, or secular version, a regimental corporatocracy, or a regimental corporate republic, homeland republic, military-homeland republic, corporate-institutional-military complex republic, of line up, then left, right, left, right, hup-hup-hup.

Of one way to think and live, a system cohomology and knot theory, mostly same-old, same-old, while behind the curtain rascals legally grab treasures; spoils, of yet another cultural war?

***

And, this toddler explores by waddling to one interesting thing after another, that includes the crown, one scepter, ornamental staff, wand, and ceremonial weapon feature after another, often pointing and touching with right index finger.

Of which, at the minimum, it seems quite rude, and at the maximum, dangerous, as some of the embedded beings are quite sensitive.

And, those sleeping beings do not want, a gentle poke, especially ones embedded in the crown, scepters, ornamental staffs, wands, and ceremonial weapons.

As many remain asleep for years, decades, some since the Edwardian era, Gilded Age, The Renaissance, Age of Discovery, Middle Ages, ancient history, Phanerozoic, Proterozoic, Archean, Hadean, and some pre-big bang.

***

In addition, all of these things seem ever so precious and rare, the crown, one scepter, ornamental staff, wand, and ceremonial weapon feature after another, with a complex interdependency, of a unique coalition.

So, breaking an irreplaceable could have serious implications.

***

And, the equal or greater point, the mother and father are nowhere in sight, or is it insight, or insigne, a missing sign, such as, "bright before me, the signs implore me?"

***

And, how can that be, the mother is nowhere in sight?

***

Such as, who would leave a toddler unattended, as it seems bizarre, and quite irresponsible.

And, a quick look about, then at a considerable distance away, laying about, a few strange beings all seem quite powerful, yet ever so weary from some unknown reason.

And again, a look about, the toddler's parents are nowhere in sight.

***

Then again, at a considerable distance, a few strange beings seem barely able to lift an arm, then seriously wave off any effort to approach this toddler and throne system, such as never ever approach, and quickly avoid this place.

Because, something happens to everyone who approaches, such as one complex thing after another, as if there is no direct path for an explorer, or platoon system, not even "one riot, one ranger."

***

And, a trespasser risks serious damage; such as, a person who would mostly sit, stare, and drool, then once in a while, have a wild-eyed-fully-animate notion, yet cannot articulate a clear line of effort; and that effort to think is filled with very active, colorful delirium, hallucinations, delusions, disorganization, and one misperception after another, about subject, verb, object, preposition, postposition, and circumposition.

Then, this trespasser's articulation would slow to a muddle, about exceptionally complex original content, about the next great Zeitgeist, or major breakthrough, in one of the major unsolved problems in physics, mathematics, chemistry, biology, medicine, theory of music, and/or all, as if the ultimate full unification theory.

***

Then, at the key revelation moment, that person would reach the great universal barrier, eyes widen, as the mind tries, and tries.

***

Then, with an indirect wide-eyed delirium, that person would rant at the wilderness, at the great frontier.

So much so, it seems as if, that person would lose one form of bearing after another, the main mental index reference points, then index of character, event, set, time, and situation.

***

Or say another way, this place creates an orphan, especially a person's frame of reference stream, vital index cues, patterns, position within time and space.

Or put another way, this person loses the central template, category, and place in mental tree.

As it seems to also orphan articles of faith, and compendium of family, friends, and social networks, the mental map of, the metabase and metadata, with all those fully indexed cues of the deep cerebral web, part of the literal and metaphorical under, midland, and overnet, especially a whitelist of exceptions, privileges, and perks, and list of the others.

So much so, this place would deliberately turn off molecular aspects, of these brain memory and failsafe neural clusters.

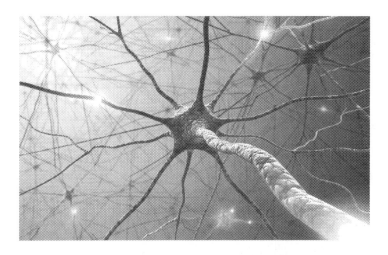

▼

PART 16, A

And at this throne system, the toddler continues to waddle about, and all the while points with right arm extended and index finger, at one elaborate throne feature after another, and each time says things in a toddler language.

Of which, most people would not understand.

And this toddler continues exploring, by waddling to one interesting thing after another, that includes the crown populated by a considerable number of supreme beings, a coalition of that also seems as if the ultimate universal and biological theater, a considerable microcosm with an experimental ecosystem, and those dynamics to sustain in some form of symbiosis, a set of persistent biological interactions maybe mutualistic, commensalistic, and parasitic.

***

And once ever so close to the crown, points with a right index finger at various world within world features, often touching parts, then touches one of the supreme beings in the belly button, and again.

***

Of which, it causes that supreme being embedded in the crown to awaken from a 419-year sleep, one that started in the year 1600, the end of the European Renaissance, because of the golden age of robber barons.

Then, this being opens eyes, smiles, and mumbles, as if quite amused, "Hmm, hmm, hmmmmm"...

... then, after careful consideration, about this and that, the head shakes, side to side, to imply that was a very rude action.

***

Then, this supreme being carefully looks left, right, above, below, back, and leans slightly forward and whispers, "Let her go."

▼

PART 16, B

Then, in an unusual language, this supreme being whispers something else, yet may have been from a song, Jools Holland & David Gray – "I Think It's Going to Rain Today."

CHAPTER 42

▼

PART 16, C

Then, this supreme being embedded in the crown, goes back to an ever so deep, delta wave sleep, as if managing something very important, such as an era, or a world within a world, or a hidden universe.

***

And, still quite curious about this throne system, the toddler explores by waddling about, examining one feature after another.

***

Then, the toddler looks beyond that system, into a nearby surrounding garden, a garden better than what one might expect within the golden age of classical and Renaissance gardens, the best of the best.

A picturesque place, with one unique garden section after another, some accessible by a hidden path.

And most sections contain colorful flowers in full bloom, shrubs, subshrubs, and distinct thematic herbal sections, a virtuous treatise of medicinal, tonic, culinary, and aromatic expressions.

Many sections sit on spectacular elevated beds.

Of which, conveys specific stages, nuisances within secular and sacred space, as in philosophical and therapeutic nuisances that cultivate, redeem, regenerate, transform, evolve, and expand, as in a place pristine, vivid, free and fair.

***

And, each place seems wholly natural, and absolutely fascinating: a place for artists, poets, scholars.

And, if need be, a place for romance, such as romance of Palamedes, or science.

***

And in each place, a person could carefully run fingers through one colorful bloom after another, then contemplate a truly great question, and another.

Then, on occasion, a person might nibble on a Raisinet, on a dark chocolate-covered raisin, and in great detail, ponder the future, such as organize thoughts.

Then notice the majestic, a panoramic view, and serene blue expanse of sky, of fresh air, such as sae fresh and fair.

Or, follow a path, and another.

Then, sit in one not-so-secret garden section after another, an st-connectivity, Risch algorithm field, a cultivated crop, a trial garden, and each garden with a microclimate substance and stylistic allure, with full potential.

And, other garden sections sit in small niches, such as inside a charming small bamboo grove, or under the full protection of a weeping willow in bloom, or between huge ceremonial boulder crops, for example an ancient rock culture, a prehistoric tribute, which forms a poetic megalithic boulder garden shrine.

***

And, all sits in a location similar to the Zhangjiajie National Forest Park, Hunan Province, China.

Yet more unusual than that, as this area contains features similar to four other places, that include Salar de Uyuni, Bolivia, and unusual polygonal fractures in sandstones, similar to a Jurassic outcrop at Grand Staircase-Escalante National Monument, bizarre rock formations in Cappadocia, Turkey, and Hoodoos formations in Bryce Canyon National Park, Inspiration Point, Utah, USA.

***

Then, the toddler looks beyond that garden system, into nearby grounds, seems curious, points that way, and mumbles toddlerism, as if explaining an interest, idea, justification, and important mission.

***

And soon, the toddler waddles out of the throne system, thru one garden section after another, often pointing at things of interest.

And eventually, the toddler waddles pass the garden outer edge, and over dangerous ground; over dirt; not typical dirt, yet the version one universally finds in religious text, and regardless of which religion, over ground that contains danger, prejudice, error, and corruption.

***

Yet, the toddler seems curious, ever so determined, points beyond, to an epic mountain range, and mumbles toddlerism that may translate into, "I'm going there to see my Father ...

"And all my loved ones who've gone on ...

"I'm just going over Jordan ...

"I'm just going over home ...

"I know dark clouds will gather 'round me ...

"I know my way is hard and steep."

CHAPTER 42

▼

PART 17

And, the toddler waddles towards that epic mountain range, then reaches a bizarre rock formation, as if to waddle beyond, then into the remote mountain range.

And, the rock outcrop has a very unusual eternal flame, a natural phenomenon produced by a natural gas leak, peat fire, or coal seam fire, of which burns, as if for an eon or more.

***

So much so, all this exploring seems quite dangerous.

And again, the equal or greater point, the mother and father are nowhere in sight, or is it insight, or insigne?

And, how can that be, the mother is nowhere in sight?

Such as, who would leave a toddler unattended, as it seems bizarre, and quite irresponsible.

And, this situation and toddler has no direct or indirect relationship to, yet may remind the reader of Natalie Merchant, "A Wayfaring Stranger" the official video with a wandering toddler.

CHAPTER 42

▼

PART 18

And meanwhile, elsewhere, about these choices inside that tunnel network, if a person tries to safely navigate within, they must avoid one wrong step or word, a script variation or tonal infraction, something not pitch-perfect, as it often leads to facticity or thrownness.

***

However, life is not perfect, nor a readily available, fully indexed script.

So much so, the tunnel system and life resembles a universal entanglement, mostly unseen science and "mythology of lost."

Because there appears no decent direct route thru this complex estate, and thru life, the universe, only a series of bad choices, a choice between bad or worse, yet based on priority swapping of dangerous alternatives, of options?

Or, the idea or option looks attractive, yet eventually arrives at series of bad choices with serious implications.

***

Again, it seems as if this tunnel complex and game are rigged.

Such as, in general, it and the universe seems "rigged," for example, all known definitions of that word.

And mostly, the system does so, as if a back-formation technique, from a built-in or inherent rigging technique, to unfold and fit an idea, situation or ship with rigging, to clothe, enhance and/or endow with special gear ...

... into a condition or position for use ...

... to detect or obey opportunity, adjust, preposition, fit, expand, fill, and that pattern ...

... for example, a beachball-sized thing expands, and expands, into a truly great container or ship ...

... rigged for something, a function, a construct for manual or automatic control ...

... and yet, rig as if one ever so temporary shelter after another, such as shelter from the last storm?

***

And inside this entire niche system, especially the tunnel, one wrong step and the system places a mark on that person, often subtle, a sound, idea, or thing, sometimes ever so grotesque with a complex entanglement, a universal preference.

Then that person or thing stumbles, or is thrown into one of these very strange and dangerous places, such as one unfortunate situation after another, often among great turbulence, such as a Rayleigh–Taylor instability, and that hydrodynamics pattern, based on the Newtonian and Hamiltonian control system.

***

Or worst yet, in this tunnel system, if a person steps on the wrong idea, place or thing, such as a stepping stone, they can be rudely thrown anywhere, and often, it seems random.

And often, thrown into an ever so danger situation, even a new life, role, and identity with a very poor memory, for example amnesia, or severely deficient autobiographical memory.

***

Or worst yet, that tunnel system can eject a person from the timeline, then history, from a category of database stubs.

***

Or say another way, entering this niche, and especially that tunnel complex, proves quite a tricky venture, as there is no direct path, no clear route thru that sphere of influence, the atmospherics. As one wrong step, and a person would trip into the theater, or flash sideways in time, or lose vital constructs, frames of reference, deep belief network, and whole categories of thought.

Or, just as importantly, gain a specie, cloaked shadow, or an entire system, just to name a few potential problems.

Or worse yet, a person or thing is instantly and rudely thrown, to the very edge of the universe, to a final frontier, then out of the universe; as a reject or rejection slip; of sail on, sail away!

CHAPTER 42

▼

PART 19, A

And, regarding that niche system, especially the main section, upon closer scrutiny of various sectors, more things seem alive, yet many do not resemble life in a classic sense, not a carbon-based life form.

As carbon represents the key component within all known life on Earth, natural life that is.

In addition, all of these internal niche walls and stacks have a considerable population of things quite difficult to describe, a microcosm or community here and there, then an occasionally strange microcosm of curiosities.

So much so, most of these internal niche things have another world aspect, primordial, yet universal.

In addition, here and there, a considerable number of strange creatures rest.

Or, a better description, they slump.

And somehow, they seem related to humans, somewhat, as in barely, yet as if progenitors.

Of which, on the whole gives an overall impression of missing links, before the golden age of sapiens, super and aquatic apes; of evolutional links much further back in time, and those major junctions of alternate biological links, scripts and solutions, yet tampered versions, what-if experiments.

***

In addition, other internal niche walls and the vault ceiling contain dense layers of bizarre *Wunderkammer.*

In fact, they resemble a *Leverian, façade* style, as dense mounted cabinets of one mystery after another, and microcosms within microcosms, categories and degrees of existence, such as crucial stages and craft from certain universal biological theater.

✷✷✷

And of equal importance, a closer look at one large odd pillar after another reveals, they often evolve here and there, highly advanced field-programmable gate arrays, mathematical objects, yet digital infinity...

..., into a mostly colorful complex, that reflect or emanate one brilliant spectrum of things and systems after another, as if various bismuth growths, a pentavalent post transition metal, pnictogens, bright silvery white fresh, pink tinge spectrum, natural diamagnetic element.

✷✷✷

Yet here, these seem far more complex, some alive, and one humanlike, or say more accurately, an elite transhuman or posthuman, yet quite groggy.

✷✷✷

And a greater question, how can someone grow a more advanced version of a human, and those tradeoffs, range of skills, prespectives?

And, at the origin of each bismuth-like thing, and bismuth for lack of a better description.

Such as, as a closer look at the standard model of known elements, a considerable number of vital and exotic elements, things, other traits, byproducts, and comparative references are missing?

PERIODIC TABLE OF THE ELEMENTS

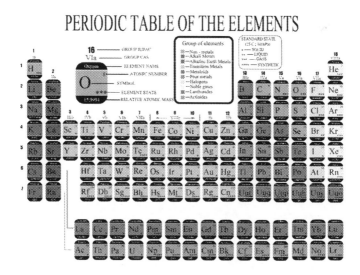

And maybe, the periodic table, also known as the periodic table of elements, a tabular display of chemical elements, is merely okay, adequate, not truly great?

As, it is not the best way to view these things, and all forms of matter in general, not the best series of comparative vantage or vista points, to a fully unified the theory of everything, a better bundle theory, other perspectives, islands of stability, islands of inversion, old and new nuclear shell model construction ways and means, old and new chemical groups, other vital indices, more accurate wave–particle duality descriptives, comprehensive traits of boundless four-dimensional continuum known as spacetime, connectional preferences of the universal and conditions in descending order, tenacity, holes that pass all the way through, and where on a P1S2all sphereism, a particle and wave contact, the preferences, the range function that includes every loop and contact point preferences?

Regardless, think simple, a table or more, that dynamically links implications, of impurities by degree, that effect, configuration, diversity, distribution patterns, function, and performance?

***

Regardless, of equal or greater importance, here and now, some of these bismuth-like things seem unmixed with any other matter, such as free from taint, dust, or dirt.

Or say another way, free from taint, as they seem spotless, stainless, free from harshness or roughness and in full accord.

***

And, of equal or greater importance, some of these bismuth-like things, and bismuth for lack of a better description seems "older than dirt, older than the Stone Age," and likely older than the universe?

***

And each, seems as if a treasure with tremendous upside potential, function, if properly fed energy and vital material at the original sweet spot.

***

And, on a nearby pillar system are a vast number of field-programmable gate arrays, programmable logic blocks, a hierarchy of reconfigurable mathematical objects interconnect, the best of the best, complex combinational functions, a superior class of automata, digital infinities, generative linguistics, origin of language, the universe.

And, carefully attached, one of these "things," a being, is slowly fed by an unusual tube system, that pulse by pulse, creates an ever so shrewd juggernaut, yet supreme crown jewel.

***

And elsewhere, thru this dense Manhattan accident crowd, a creature arrives, not visible, undetectable, has no mass, and seems to take up no space, no volume, yet emits a considerable amount of unique gravitons, and "exotic forms" of dark energy.

Then, this creature, a farmer, yet some may say the framer, quickly studies one elite crowd member after another, especially from the University of Tokyo, Japan, and lingers there.

***

Then, with a device, ever so carefully inspects this person, head to toe, scans the cell phone content, prefrontal cortex and thalamus, yet notices a few serious brain anomalies, life-threatening, adjusts the device settings, then quickly repairs these regions of the brain, and quietly moves to an elite member of the Defense Advanced Research Projects Agency (DARPA), then ETH Zürich, Pierre and Marie Curie University.

And pauses at a person from the University of Copenhagen, carefully inspects this person from head to toe, scans the cell phone content, prefrontal cortex and thalamus, and finds no serious anomalies, life-threatening, then scans a nearby shadow cabinet member.

CHAPTER 42

▼

PART 19, B

Yet more interesting, next to this person is a young Japanese woman with serious medical problems, terminal, weeks to live, yet she deliberately hides it from others.

And, of equal or greater interest, after a brief electronic device scan, she also has an unusual physiology, somewhat like a genetic chimera, a person with distinct genotypes, a mixed collection of DNA in different regions of the body, and from biological inheritance of the mother, and father.

Yet with a further electronic device scan, it quickly becomes quite apparent, some regions are materials from each grandparent, great-grandparent, great-great-grandparent, and further back, as many as ten or more generations.

Such as, how is this possible?

And, another more detailed electronic scan, reveals this young woman seems to have the greatest known DNA collection, a mixed literal and metaphorical, a morphometric that discloses the Japanese evolution process.

And of equal note, her heart DNA is Western, from a Scandinavian, and not a transplant, yet brain and remaining body is 100 percent Japanese.

Such as, how is this possible?

And, her collection of Japanese DNA, seems as if a compelling history of the Japanese people.

Yet, one of her ancestors was a Westerner, an explorer, a sapien, European early modern human, during the most dramatic rise, an Age of Discovery, especially the legendary island of Japan, *Nippon, Nippon-kokum,* or *Nihon-koku,* a State of Japan!

***

So, this stealth creature carefully studies the device database, then applies another search algorithm, and another, then concludes, she is an ultrarare human, quite, yet terminally ill, with weeks to live from an unrelated illness.

Then, the undetectable creature makes a very serious mistake, moves closer, and closer to this Japanese woman, looks carefully into her eyes, then her lips quiver, and quiver, then her other feelings arrive of serious regret, warm tears, and true pathos beyond a full description.

***

Then elsewhere, embedded in an utmost crown, it causes that same supreme being, to awaken from a 419-year sleep, a sleep that started in the year 1600, the end of the European Renaissance, because of the golden age of robber barons.

And, this being whispers, "Let her go."

***

And, of equal or greater significance, this young Japanese woman seems quite lonely, as many Japanese people are, and mostly exhausted, from work, and must *inemuri,* the Japanese art of sleeping in public, anywhere, anytime, even at work, from a very long workday, day after day, week after week, for years.

And all risk a serious circadian dysfunction, maybe a depersonalization disorder, or risk a profound mental break, and quite possibly, although rare, a Capgras delusion, of which a person holds a delusion that a friend, spouse, parent, or other close family member, and pets, have been replaced by an identical-looking impostor, a delusional misidentification syndrome, and/or that time has been warped, or somehow shifted, or clipped.

Then, this creature scans this Japanese woman, and notices her cell salts distribution, also called mineral salts, or tissue salts, and lack of in some cases, or seems incorrect, region by bodily region.

And, this creature wonders another very serious question, why some Japanese pensioners want to go to jail, and why the Japan's Princess Ayako surrenders her royal title, as if from the cumulative stress and tremendous pressure so many Japanese feel, of tremendous scrutiny, of trapped yet again, as a truly knotted object, a principled bundle.

And regarding, this very lonely young Japanese woman, once she is gone, will anyone miss her?

Will they truly miss her?

And, before the very end, will she cry?

Will she weep in a final purifying-cleanse, of a good cry, a final, deep, and profound cry, to cleanse the mind, body, and soul?

Will she release all of those powerful emotions; finally release them, and lips quiver, and quiver, to release that heavy burden?

Will warm tears flow?

Will they purify her, redeem her, and will the lower lip quiver, and quiver?

▼

PART 19, C

And again, this undetectable creature makes a serious mistake, moves closer, and closer to this young Japanese woman looks carefully into her eyes, then her lips quiver, and quiver, then her other feelings arrive, of serious regret, warm tears, and true pathos beyond all known description.

***

So much so, this creature realizes, *If she dies, I die.*

***

Then, this creature electronically scans her again, seriously considers possibilities and implications, the benefits and risks, the up and down size.

As meddling in this special case would have ever so serious implication, especially to the Japanese people, their future.

Primarily because the adjustment technique to her, would alter her DNA system, that unusually rare coalition, then have profound implications.

The adjustments to her, would also propel a gene or more throughout the Japanese population, that dilemma.

***

And again, this undetectable creature makes a serious mistake, looks carefully into her eyes, then her lips quiver, and quiver, then her other feelings arrive, of serious regret, warm tears, and true pathos beyond description.

***

So much so, this creature realizes, *If she dies, I die.*

***

As it may represent, an unseen interconnection, an entanglement, such as a single thread could snag, cause an entanglement, as if a universal phenomenon, a minor thing could create a major event.

For example, regarding this young Japanese with a terminal illness, could trip on a sidewalk edge, and bump into others, and that chain of events.

And moments later, this young Japanese angel stumbles, falls, awkwardly regains balance, yet her cell phone flips about, then eventually impact on the ground, that triggers the cell phone media player to start a song, such as Cold Mountain, "Like a Songbird That Has Fallen"?

CHAPTER 42

▼

PART 19, D

Meanwhile, this creature studies one computerized scenario after another, then again, and seriously agonizes over the big data dilemma, the analytics, of ever so subtle analytic–synthetic distinctions, such as the big data dilemma, data sets, the "Accumulo NoSQL of the metabase" with real-time data streams that monitor data heaps, which unfortunately create the metacircular paradox, from so much stuff, probabilities, as it creates a trouble tree for every known complex system.

So much so, this problem, to save her, fix the medical problems, has many bad choices, a major dilemma, a quandary, catch-22, Cornelian dilemma, or Pyrrhic victory-based system.

***

And again, regarding this woman, the creature makes another tremendous mistake, and closely looks in her eyes, and has sympathy, then a profound sense of empathy, and realizes, *If she dies, I die.*

***

Then, the creature picks her most stable DNA, points that electronic devices at her, deactivates some genes, knockout others, activates others, reinforces the immune system, recovery time ability, and repairs her caudate nucleus, a control system that manages various thresholds, potentials, memories, goals, and especially improves her ability to truly fall in love.

***

Then, this creature goes to knockout a few genes that nearly everyone has, a set of, the great pretender, fakeness, and ever so sly.

Yet she has none of those genes.

As omnivores have a treacherous personality component, mode of thinking, the highest form of treason, especially a relative morality system, relative to the temporal inflection, the media/medium of the moment, day, and week, and from serving too many masters.

And, unfaithful to civility, a true meritocracy.

And often, offer a huge discount to a gender, tribe, team, religion, race, state, such as, to grade on very steep curve, a huge discount, for members, for legacy offspring, compared to a true meritocracy.

Yet she has none of those genes.

Then, this creature goes to activate a few genes, that promotes cool, calm, civil, genuine, reasonable, and methodical.

Yet hers are active.

Then, this creature, goes to deactivate a few genes, that promote cronyism, and desperate to mimic a situation, someone more than willing, to if need be, turn coldblooded, a lack of mercy, and more than willing to sacrifice something, a person, idea, principle, philosophy, and system.

Yet, the creature finds none of those genes, nor genes that create drama and divisiveness.

▼

PART 19, E

Then, this creature activates a few more genes, that fortify more immune system techniques, processes, other nuances, and list of gaps between each one.

***

Yet, all these DNA and other modifications will have other very serious implications, as this person's appearance, personality, and habits would greatly change, and some people may soon, in the next few weeks, see her as the Mother of Japan, *Nippon, Nippon-kokum,* or *Nihon-koku,* a polymath, renaissance humanism, gifted in the classics, earth, space, life, physical, formal sciences, and with long-flowing blond, curling hair, emerald blue eye, quite Japanese, a quintessential yet with a Scandinavian heart.

And moments later, this creature, or being without mass, carefully looks about this dense Manhattan accident crowd, one sector at a time, north, east, south, west, above, then towards the earth's rolling direction, then the North Star, and moments later, looks elsewhere in the sky, to city on the edge of forever.

✻✻✻

And quickly, in this dense Manhattan accident crowd, smells arrives, of pine, cedar, and storax.

Then moments later, in this dense Manhattan accident crowd, the creature notices, carefully looks about, scans with a device, finds nothing, then ever so quietly moves to the Swedish Academy committee secretary, examines, especially the cell phone details, then permanent seasoned adviser well known in Scandinavia as "the specialist," a cultural linguistic specialist, often called upon for knowledge about specific candidate skillsets, clarity, efficiency, effectiveness, realism and ability to reveal nature.

✻✻✻

And moments later, the creature carefully looks about for danger, locates Gus, who seems quite preoccupied, especially with a person that wears *Østmo* Service Boots.

Then quietly, the creature slips a note into the Nobel Committee member's pocket.

And moments later, from that same Committee member, a different pocket, this creature quietly removes a small red envelope, handwritten by the member in thirteen languages including Navaho, *Dispilio*, Linear A, *Cascajal* Block, *Quipu*, *Rongorongo*, and two poetic *aristo* yet cryptic languages, and not a shallow language-game, as each is a serious peer-reviewable dereistic.

And, the final part of this handwritten note seems untranslatable, yet the thematics hints at Graham Nash "Better Days?"

▼

PART 19, F

AND YET ANOTHER A COMMERCIAL BREAK: SON OF DAVE "AIN'T GOIN' TO NIKE TOWN"?

CHAPTER 42

▼

Part 19, G

Intermission: Son of Dave, "Going for
Ice, Everyone Back to My Hotel, Ep1"?

▼

Part 20, H

Intermission, and a different party, yet, everyone is invited, Shaggy featuring Chaka Khan "Get my party on"?

CHAPTER 42

▼

Part 19, I

And yet another a commercial break

Good morning.

My name is Nestor Boholst Bande, editor of this new book series, *The Valet, aka The Adventures of Will Ferrell and the Scandinavian,* and every book series written by Bryan Fletcher, born in Princeton, New Jersey, USA, the *Legend of the Mighty Sparrow,* and *Another Runaway Bride.*

***

Yet please forgive me, as Bryan rarely follows my editorial advice about spelling, punctuation, grammar, ideas, characterizations, sets, settings, style, thematics, and other novel writing components of the storytelling system, the "physical system," monomyth, "Talent and Taste," "*Snille och Smak,*" the primary purpose; to further the purity, strength, and fully reveal the aesthetics of nature, the universe, to explore one branch after another, such as science, art, beauty, taste, and especially the sublime features of life and language; the ability to accurately communicate, a well-crafted mastery of language, such as the ways and means to communicate and reveal a culture; especially the practical and aesthetics of science, art, beauty, and the sublime; to reveal one mystery of existence after another, and often, what appears as if an untranslatable idea, character, function, setting, or system;

of something "beyond all language and thought, and beyond all categories of being, is it, or is it not?"

***

To offer a compelling story, and/or, a "high concept" page turning adventure, often misadventure, of one compelling perspective or angle after another with a profound thematic structure.

***

Or say another way, the ways and means to free a person and nation; the ultimate prize, to recover and improve the culture, into the best version of a truly great society.

***

And, do things evolve, and eventually mature?

Does the literary work carefully explore one relationship after another, and at any given moment, in great depth, such as to study a people, organization, place, condition, time, and sequence?

Does the work show purpose, cause, effect, results, and show historical context, such as to the human species, a history of, and the universe?

***

And, the novel needs to communicate in a clear, organized, concise, accurate, grammatically correct, persuasive manner, and, on occasion, with an extraordinary style, elegance, and charm; to reveal true human potential, such as an ability to seamlessly flow, as if a virtuoso; with a certain flow, rhythm, style, wit, and *panache;* especially as it relates to the classic problematic situation of people, and social systems; a spiral of silence, cycle of poverty, *Vicious Circle* by Jacek Malczewski, self-fulfilling prophecy; or a dense literal and metaphorical forest filled with thorny brier extensions, of same-old, same-old, of life as a lowly trope or "redshirt," a disposable stock character or disposable species.

Does the literary work, or work in general show clarity, efficiency, effectiveness, realism and ability to reveal nature?

Yet the writer, Bryan Fletcher, rarely accepts these fundamental principles.

In fact, without my permission, he edited this commercial break; deleted and added things.

So again, please accept my sincere apology.

NESTOR BOHOLST BANDE

Facebook Address: https://www.facebook.com/lotusgreen2017/

Linkedin Profile: https://www.linkedin.com/in/nestor-boholst-bande-6959993b/

1. Services Offered:

    - Proofreading
    - Mechanical Editing
    - Substantial Editing
    - Developmental Editing
    - Content Writing: Technology (SaaS, AI, Machine Learning, Digital Trends), Lifestyle, Politics, Society, History, Science, etc.

2. Favorite Sayings:

- The life we all live is amateurish and accidental; it begins in accident and proceeds by trial and errors and toward dubious ends. That is the law of nature. But the dream of man will not accept what nature hands us. We have to tinker with it, trying to give it purpose, direction, and meaning— or, if we are of another mind, trying to demonstrate that life has no purpose, direction, or meaning. Either way, we can't let it alone. The unexamined life, as the wise Greek said, is not worth living. We have to examine it, if only to persuade ourselves that we matter and are in control, or that we are at least aware of what is being done to us. (Wallace Stegner/ John Cheever)
- Shake off all the fears of servile prejudices, under which weak minds are servilely crouched. Fix reason firmly in her seat, and call on her tribunal for every fact, every opinion. Question with boldness even the existence of a God because, if there be one, he must more approve of the homage of reason than that of blindfolded fear. (Thomas Jefferson)
- The only way that we can live is if we grow. The only way we can grow is if we change. The only way we can change is if we learn. The only way we can learn is if we are exposed. And the only way that we are exposed is if we throw ourselves into the open." (C. Joybell)
- In life, if you don't risk anything, you often risk everything.
- From your mistakes, you can often learn great things, when you are not busy denying them.
- A person is more of, what that person hides and their collective biome preference yet often hides from that person, as compared to what a person thinks, wears, gestures, and says.
- A person, does not have to be wrong, for the other person to be right; that dichotomy, only a black or white choice, a binary thinking system, ever so flat, not multidimensional,

ability to fold space, time, and options in complex ways and means; as both may be correct, or correct in varying degrees.

- The smallest act of kindness, can have a profound effect, magnification, and may generate more worth more than the grandest intention, and eloquent speech?
- Many people are quite poor, because the only thing they have is money.
- Everything you think, gesture and say, becomes part of your past, present and future.
- If you lie, it becomes a debt.

3. Philosophy to live by: I am, therefore I survey, consider a full spectrum of ideas, remember, compare, assign value, prioritize, index, evolve, plan, reconsider, improve, prioritize, plan, deploy, adjust, and try to grow wiser with each interaction.

4. Consider Wallace Earle Stegner, American novelist, short story writer, environmentalist, historian, said "The Dean of Western Writers," especially explorers of the novel system; and if interested, the Pulitzer Prize for Fiction nominees, and other exceptional ideas, people, systems, high cultural award systems, and fresh air.

Thank you, and have a nice day. ☺

Nestor Boholst Bande

PS: Bryan put that happy face icon, as no classic literary editor would do so; as it breaks the formal editing regimental protocol system, as compared to a "novel" writing system; Middle English, from Anglo-French, new, from Latin *novellus*."

"Two, three, four!"

ABOUT THE AUTHOR

Born in Princeton, New Jersey, Bryan Fletcher is a fiction adventure nerd, who writes survivor genre, especially a down and out hero against all odds, against powerful special interests too-big-to-fail; a system controlled by ultimate insiders; who often seem hell-bent on trivial pursuit, obsession, the last war, escalation, cruel and usual.

***

So we live according to them, their concerns or lack of, that style of raising a family, a system without substantial peer review checks and balances...

... those vital safety features...

... those vital traits to live a cool, calm, balanced, reasonable, interesting, and sustainable life.

**

So here we are, a new book series, *The Valet, aka The Adventures of Will Ferrell and the Scandinavian.*

Author e-mail and Facebook address:
bfletch157@yahoo.com

Postal Address:
2560 Hemlock Farms, Lords Valley, PA, USA, 18428

Supporting websites:

https://anotherrunawaybride.com/

http://legendofthemightysparrow.com/

Printed in the United States
By Bookmasters